WARPED WOMEN

Also by J.T. Pritchard aka Janet Pritchard
Lady Cop
One Hot Night
Sin Ship
Stationwagon Wives

WARPED WOMEN

J.T. PRITCHARD

CUTTING EDGE

ISBN-13: 978-1-957868-59-2

Published by
Cutting Edge Books
PO Box 8212
Calabasas, CA 91372
www.cuttingedgebooks.com

CHAPTER ONE

"WILL you please stop pushing against me that way? Now, please!"

The morning subway rush was slightly past its peak. But, caught in the moist press of over-warm bodies at one end of an uptown car, Cynthia Bennett, age nineteen, was too recent a newcomer to New York to appreciate that fact.

She saw the trains as monsters out of some surrealist fragment of delirium, each one a many-mouthed dragon, alternately devouring and spewing out victims. The teeming platform crowd, fighting and snarling against itself, both frightened and angered her. It formed a shapeless, viscous herd bulging suicidally into the iron jaws which hissed insanely as they chopped it to pieces. Nothing in her background had been designed to prepare her for the mob's naked hatred of itself, the individual's bullying offensiveness when wearing a mask of anonymity. That was one of the things she had not been taught at Miss Thatcher's Finishing School for Young Ladies.

Crushed against the steel wall of the car's platform, Cynthia closed her eyes and tried to draw her mind away from the unpleasant sensation of being rocked back and forth by the bodies about her as the car swayed. The large man on her right leaned heavily upon her with each motion, seeming to make no effort to avoid pressing his elbow against the taut swell of Cynthia's pent, breathless body; seeming, if anything, to maintain that pressure even when the motion of the car should have moved him away from her. Once she opened her eyes to find him looking sidelong at the revealing lines of her sweater which, she now realized, had shrunk when last laundered. She attempted a glare but it was, finally, her own eyes which wavered and turned away. Somehow she never knew just what to do when people stared at her—and they stared frequently.

She was the sort of girl that people just naturally look at. For one thing, her coloring was an oddly vibrant combination of deep brown eyes, tawny blonde hair and a clear, rather dark skin which tanned without freckling. But there were other reasons—several reasons, and all having to do with shapeliness where a girl should be shapely and slimness where a girl should be slim, and of these reasons the most outstanding were—well, outstanding.

And Cynthia knew, in an objective way, that she was pretty—or perhaps something more than pretty. She had, in fact, quite honestly included that in her mental list of assets when she decided to stop pretending that her putterings about in her father's office were of any value to him or to her own peace of mind, and had come to New York, only days ago, to try to find out how and where she really fitted in the scheme of things...

The man beside her rudely interrupted her thoughts.

He seemed to be trying to dig something from his topcoat pocket. Through the material of his coat she could feel his hand move searchingly back and forth. Cynthia felt her skin crawl. She opened her mouth, but somehow could not scream. After all, probably the man was not even thinking of her, was not even aware of her existence... It was her own imagination, her own twisted soul, making her attach significance even to perfectly innocent actions, so long as they were male actions. She knew that about herself, yet could not help it. Could not help shrinking from all contact, could not help imagining all sorts of dangers whenever men were near. This subway with its press of bodies was torture. This man next to her, his hand moving in his coat pocket—Cynthia took a deep breath, then suddenly laughed. Of course; all innocent! The man had suddenly come up with the thing he had been digging for, a pocket digest of some sort; he flipped the pages and settled into it, holding on to a strap with one hand.

Though relieved, Cynthia made a mental promise to herself that, if she got any sort of job from the employment agency she was now on her way to call on, she would ride the bus to work rather than the subway.

The train screamed to a shuddering stop, and Cynthia found herself being buffeted about as a part of the crowd inside the car charged against those outside and battled them for use of the doorway. Spun in the eddy of that boiling turbulence, Cynthia was turned so that she pressed face to face against the man with the magazine. She put her hands against a door post to hold herself back as much as possible, but her strength was not equal to the task. She was flung indelicately upon the other, and as more people crammed into the car she was wedged there, unable to move away.

Over the top of the magazine, the man's eyes looked down at her. She could not see the rest of his face, but her own was flushing a bright pink. She tried to balance her body against the car's crazy rocking as it picked up speed. Then she felt his hand move. Creep stealthily back into his pocket. Cynthia's mouth formed an "O" of mingled astonishment and outrage, but no sound came forth. The man's eyes looked blankly at her, then returned to his book as though he were completely unaware of her. But his hand remained in his pocket, bulging knuckles digging into Cynthia as the train swayed. This time she was really about to scream— but the hand came out of the pocket, holding a handkerchief, with which the man casually mopped his red, sweating face.

The train slid screeching to a bone-jarring stop. Swallowing her scream, and a lump of disgust, Cynthia slid shamefacedly out of the car exit as the doors opened, propelled by the surging crowd behind her. This thing inside her, this fear, this hurt—it was destroying her. She was beginning to make a fool of herself. That poor man. He hadn't done a thing, actually; yet if she had screamed he would have been arrested, or at very least put in a position of terrible embarrassment. Cynthia's face was still a rich pink as she climbed the stairs to sunny Forty-second Street and started walking briskly toward the address of the employment agency.

"Name?"

"Cynthia Bennett."

The pen raced easily across the form-card.

"Age?"

"Nineteen."

"Sex—definitely."

Cynthia's brows wrinkled in puzzlement. The woman behind the desk caught the expression and smiled.

"Definitely female," she explained.

Cynthia flushed slightly as she glanced down at the tight-drawn sweater beneath her suit jacket.

"I shouldn't have tried to wash it myself," she said. "Is it really as bad as that?"

"It's not bad at all. It's..." The woman sighed as she eyed the bodice of her own chic blouse. "It's darned unfair, though." She flicked the card with her finger, and on the highly polished desk top it spun like a marker in some game of chance. When it stopped she straightened it out and absently spun it again.

"Tell me something about yourself, Cynthia," she said. "Oh, I've read the resume form you filled out. But I can learn a lot more about a girl this way, get a better idea of what kind of a job she can handle best, so that both she and the employer are satisfied."

There seemed so very little to tell, thought Cynthia.

But your name was Cynthia Bennett, and you went to the County Day School at Spragton instead of P. S. 38, and then, because your family didn't want you to be a nasty little snob, you tried Central High—but not Tech, obviously—for six months before you cornered your father in his study one evening and convinced him that you really should be going to private school along with most of the girls you'd grown up with. So for the next three and a half years it was Piercely-Oakes, and then a finishing year at Miss Thatcher's... where *that* happened...

"Finishing school where, Cynthia?" prompted the woman who was interviewing her. Cynthia suddenly realized that she had fallen silent.

"Miss Thatcher's. When I was through there I tried to help out in Daddy's office, but I'm afraid I was just in the way. Finally I began to feel as though I weren't of much use—to myself or anybody else. I—but I'm talking too much. You don't want to hear about things like this."

The interviewer reached for a cigaret, offered one to Cynthia, and blew out a gust of smoke toward the ceiling.

"I hear all sorts of stories in this job," she said. "I can finish yours for you right now. You decided that you were going to do something useful with your life. You have no particular training, you've never had a real job, you haven't prepared yourself even to the extent of learning what might be expected of you in any job. But you're willing to learn, you're not afraid of work, and you're sure that somewhere in New York City there must be a job which will make it possible for you at least to support yourself while you find out where you belong in the scheme of things. In the meantime you'll do anything."

She paused. Cynthia said soberly, "I'm afraid that's just about it."

"Anything," the woman repeated after a moment. "Do you have any idea of how many girls come to this city and wind up doing just that? Anything. Everything. Oh, don't bother to protest. I know you're not that kind of a girl. It couldn't happen to you. Somebody else. Always somebody else." She rapped her cigaret against the tray. "Now I am going to go through a little ritual. Trains leave Penn Station every few minutes. One of them is going to your home town. My advice is to lift that phone at your elbow and arrange to be on it. While you are thinking it over, I want you to think about something else. I have your card on my desk. Thousands of others have lain there before yours. I have a few hundred blanks waiting in my desk, there are several thousands more waiting in that steel cabinet against the wall, and the printer knows he has a standing order for more, just as long as this place is in business. What happens to them?"

She nodded toward two metal trays. One held half a dozen cards: the other was already spilling over.

"One of those," she said, "is a live pile. People I'm pretty sure of placing. The others—" She shrugged. "We file them for a few weeks."

"And my card goes into the big pile," said Cynthia.

"What else can I do with it?" the woman asked. "What can you offer an employer? You've been brought up to be—a lady, I guess. Cynthia, frankly, what do you think you can do?"

"I hoped I'd be able to model. Fashions, I mean. If I can't do anything else," she went on with a trace of bitterness, "I could at least stand still while I was being photographed. I have a reasonably good figure, and I know good clothes and how to wear them. And my coloring photographs well."

The other looked her over appraisingly.

"Blonde hair—brown eyes. An unusual combination when it's natural. Dark skin—you tan rather than freckle, don't you? And with your figure... yes, I suppose it's a possibility. But this isn't a modeling agency. And unless you're one of the lucky few on top, it's one of the hardest ways I know of making a living. Those girls you see running around with hatboxes—don't think they're all models. One out of ten, yes. The rest wish they were. One agency after another, all day long, waiting for that lucky break... Are you going to use that phone, Cynthia?"

Cynthia shook her head.

"I must seem awfully silly and stubborn," she said. "I know you are right in everything you've told me, and I understand better now just what the odds are against me. But I'm not afraid of long chances. Look at the odds against ever being born in the first place! I'll just keep on looking."

She began gathering her purse and gloves. The woman spread her hands in a wry expression of defeat, then held up a restraining finger while she flipped through a card index.

"There's just one thing here that you might possibly fit into. A jet-propelled beauty salon. One of those Fifth Avenue places that makes you lovely in two weeks, ravishing in a month, and irresistible in ninety days. A sort of fancy training camp for millionaire matrons from what I've heard. They want someone to help out with the gym course. No hairdressing or anything like that. Physical conditioning. Your application said something about camp counselling…"

"Oh yes," Cynthia said eagerly. "I was Senior Counsellor in Physical Ed. during my last two years at summer camp. Swimming instructor, games organizer—and I studied dancing with Leah Telfer for two seasons. That ought to help."

"It might. Well, it's a long shot. I don't know much about the place myself, but if you want to take a chance…"

Ten minutes later Cynthia was on her way to the *House of Cimier*, a note of introduction in her purse.

CHAPTER TWO

I T was a beautiful spring morning, but as Cynthia swung lightly along Forty-second Street toward the bus stop, she hardly noticed that. Her mind was too busy turning over the things she must remember to say to her prospective employer.

J. Carter, the card said. John, probably. Certainly nothing as Gallic-sounding as the name of the place itself. But what kind of a man would he be? What sort of a man went into the business of trimming up too-soft female bodies, repairing the ravages of laziness and self-indulgence? One of those gushy, arty types with petulant spells of temperament?

There'd be classes in calisthenics, of course. That would be easy. She'd gotten over that first, self-conscious embarrassment in directing groups. And she *was* good at athletics. At home she had a little collection of ribbons, trophies—high-diving, track, riding...

Riding!

Like a loosed reptilian thing surging up from a slimy ooze, the unwanted thought slithered into her mind. She saw, with an inner eye, a familiar horse-barn, distorted shadow-figures cast by the yellow light of a lantern. The beady glint of a hungry stare. The slack mouth splitting a drunken face in a triumphant leer. In her nostrils she sensed again the mingled sweetness of hay, the ammoniac odor of the restive horses, the stale sweat-smell of the hard body pressed roughly against hers.

She felt suddenly ill, and stopped in her tracks. She was passing the library, and the little park behind it gestured invitingly.

Benches, pigeons, budding trees. She turned up the steps that led into it, paused a moment at the water fountain, and found an unoccupied bench.

"I won't think about it," she told herself. "If I just don't think about it, it will go away. It was two hundred miles from here. And it didn't happen. *It didn't happen!*"

But it was happening now. Happening all over again. Happening here in the bright sunlight of Manhattan's Bryant Park, with thousands of people hurrying obliviously by on the nearby street. And nothing she could do would stop it. She clutched her purse until her knuckles whitened, leaned back on the bench. Her eyes closed, and it possessed her. Possessed her as completely as it sometimes did at night, when she was over-tired or upset. She was back at Miss Thatcher's ...

She was back at Miss Thatcher's near the end of her last term. Marge, her roommate, was home for a few days, and she had the place to herself. The radio was on, turned low, and from halfway across the country a dance orchestra played a nostalgic medley of tunes. She felt restless, lonely, somehow.

She was too alert to sleep, and too preoccupied to study. And she'd had a rough day. A calling-down for not having finished a French essay due that morning. Then, at lunch, that excitable Johnson girl, the one whose eyes looked so angrily at the world, raising the roof over an expensive scatter-pin she'd lost. Practically accusing the whole table of having stolen it. Finally Flame, the red-bay who was Cynthia's favorite, had bolted during riding class, carrying her almost a half-mile with the bit in his teeth before she regained mastery. The rest of the girls had been excited about that, of course, and when they got back to the stable, Jake, the new hostler, had handled Flame pretty roughly.

Cynthia's mind kept dwelling on Flame. It wasn't like him to bolt. And there was something wrong about Jake. Something cruel and vindictive in the way he managed the animals. If Jake had been mistreating Flame, that could explain the horse turning ugly. Or it might be something as simple as a galling sore that Jake hadn't noticed or didn't care about.

She glanced at her watch. It was well after hours. No one was supposed to be out of the house at this time without a pass from the house mother. But if she didn't leave the grounds it wouldn't matter. Just a rule stretched a point or two. A walk should help her sleep, quiet this restlessness. And, if she went past the stables and stopped for a minute or two, she might find out what was bothering Flame.

Going to her bureau, she probed through her things until she unearthed a small flashlight. She hesitated over a light cardigan, then decided against it. The night was warm enough to make her shorts and halter adequate.

Her rubber-soled sneakers were silent on the stairs.

Stars were flung across a black velvet sky as though by a prodigal, good-spirited giant. Peepers were singing their hopeful, high-pitched love songs down by the swamp. The soft grass along the darkened path Cynthia chose was lightly dampened with a touch of dew. About her she felt the thousand eyes of night, curiously watching her. Nocturnal voices questioned as she approached, fell silent as she passed, then tentatively took up their querulous gossiping behind her. Without using the light, she picked her way as much by instinct as by sight across the grounds toward the out-buildings, now and then catching the reflected shimmer of stars in the nearby pond, being startled once or twice by a sudden, popping splash as some heavy bass or pickerel swirled up to take a frog or a struggling moth.

At the open door of the stable she spoke softly, calling the horses by name, for she knew the panic that could spread among them if she walked in silently, blinding them with a light. Using the flash in such a way that it glowed as much on her as on the animals, she made her way to Flame's stall. Still talking, she gave him her hand to sniff, stroked his nose, then laid her palm firmly on his neck. Climbing lightly over the front of the stall, she dropped beside him.

Within moments she knew the explanation for Flame's actions that afternoon. The animal's mouth was raw, ripped cruelly by a heavy curb bit that must have been edged. Jake's work, without a doubt, for he liked to ride Flame when he was on some errand about the grounds. It went with his style of riding, his habit of dragging a horse down to its haunches from a full gallop.

She slapped Flame's shoulder sympathetically.

"We'll take care of that, boy," she promised. "No more curb bits for you, if I have to steal them all and drop them in the pond."

She reached into the feeding trough for a wisp of hay, her fingers slipping into a covered corner which the horse could not reach. Suddenly something stung her, wasplike, and with an exclamation she yanked her hand away. A droplet of blood seeped from her fingertip. She turned the light downward on something that glittered and sparkled from its hiding place in a wide crack between two boards. She dug at it with her nail, brought it out. It was the Johnson girl's scatter-pin. Then Flame snorted, his splendid head jerking angrily upward...

Jake stood looking at her, one hand holding a flickering oil lantern, the other balled into a fist and jammed belligerently on his hip.

"Caught you with the goods, eh?" he said. "Thought you had a real safe place to hide it, down here in the stable, didn't you? Now don't tell me that *ain't* Miss Johnson's pin. I seen her wearing it. Just this morning, in fact, before all the fuss was made about it."

Cynthia's first gasp of surprise turned into an exclamation of outrage.

"You must be out of your mind," she said. "Of course it's Miss Johnson's pin. I just found it here in Flame's feed box."

"Oh, just *found* it, did we? Well ain't that cute, now. Just *happened* to be passing by in the middle of the night, just *happened* to put our hand in the feed box, and there it was, by jingo!"

Cynthia clutched the pin and light in one hand and scrambled over the stall again. There was no fear in her—just a burning, sick rage at the unwashed lout who stood grinning at her, openly ogling her tapering bare thighs as she poised for the short drop downward. Facing him squarely, she said,

"I intend to report this entire incident tomorrow morning. First, I intend to have you brought up for mistreatment of the animals in your care. Secondly, I shall let it be known that you have insulted me and accused me of theft. Thirdly, I shall report that you were wandering about the stable drunk and carrying an oil lamp."

Jake's free hand shot out like a striking copperhead and grasped her wrist, twisting it until both flashlight and pin dropped at his feet.

"Aw, I wouldn't do that if I was you," he grinned. "I don't think it would be smart at all. Because if I thought you was going to do that, I'd just have to call up the Dean's place right away and tell her I caught a dirty little crook sneakin' around the stable. All I'd have to do would be tell just what I saw. In half an hour you'd be squirming like a worm on a hook."

"Let me go! You must be insane!"

"*I* must, huh? Well, I wouldn't know about that. From what I hear, that pin cost over a hundred dollars. And a certain young stuck-up, they tell me, was sitting right next to Miss Johnson just about the time she missed it. Not that any of Miss Thatcher's girls would *steal* mind you. They got a fancier name when somebody like them gets caught. Klepto-something. Means they're a little bit crazy. Means you can't depend on hardly anything they say."

He reached up with one hand and hung the lantern on a nail. The horses stirred restively in their stalls.

"Now I *might* be made to believe it was all just something I dreamed. Maybe I didn't see a light in here. Maybe—" He chuckled at a sudden new thought and went on, "Maybe, when he heard me coming, some young punk from the college didn't tear out of here draggin' his britches in one hand. Maybe I didn't find a girl gallivantin' around as if she was crazy, trying to hide a pin he was supposed to help her get rid of. Maybe she didn't offer me something to forget it, before I made her shut her dirty mouth and marched her up to the Dean. Maybe."

His tongue flicked out over his dry lips. His eyes ran over Cynthia's body from head to toe, eagerly underlining the too-clear meaning of the word, *"maybe"*. Quickly, then, he dragged her toward him, one arm around her waist crushing her thinly-clad hips, her straining thighs, to himself. Her heaving flesh was flattened against his bruising chest. She freed one arm and, sobbing dryly, struck him across the bridge of the nose.

He released her, and she flung herself toward the door, but before she had taken two steps his fist caught her brutally across the back of the neck. She stumbled to her knees, too stunned to cry out. Then his hands wrapped into the back of her halter, twisting until her breasts felt bursting from the pressure. He shook her as he might have shaken a kitten, pulling her to her feet. And at that moment, sensing the mastery of his strength, Cynthia finally felt fear.

"Don't! Please don't," she begged as he spun her about.

Very deliberately he stepped back and hit her. She fell again, spinning as she went down. A hand knotted into her hair, yanking her head sharply back. His open palm sounded like pistol shots on her face. Whimpering, she rocked on her knees in front of him.

"Over there," he ordered in an odd, choked voice. "Quick. Now."

He gestured toward a pile of hay in one corner. Cynthia looked up at his face and saw death staring back at her. Dazedly she half stumbled, was half-carried, to the dark spot. His shadow loomed giantlike and swaying on the rafters overhead just before she closed her eyes. What happened after that was the substance of which nightmares are woven.

"What's the matter, pigeon, not enough sleep last night?"

The insinuating voice brought her back to reality, to the little park, to the sunlight. A pimply faced youth, overdressed in the flashy style of the wolf-packs which roam midtown Manhattan, had seated himself next to her on the bench. Cynthia's eyes narrowed contemptuously. She stood up and walked back toward the street. The youth sat looking after her, watching her hips.

"Nifty," he said appreciatively to himself.

Cynthia boarded an uptown bus, paid her fare and found a seat. Automatically her eyes watched the street numbers, but her mind still struggled to push back those memories which it could never obliterate. The terror of those next few days while she waited in hopeless dread for her shame to be somehow discovered and made public. Waited for someone to question her about the flashlight, which she had left along with the pin when she finally had crept, face in hands, back into the night. Then the dreams, in which she lived through the whole nauseating horror again and again and again. Finally, her conversation with the Johnson girl as they were walking from a class. Though she knew it was foolhardy to bring up the subject, Cynthia could not keep herself from asking about the pin.

"I haven't found it," said the girl shortly. "And I don't suppose I will, in a place like this."

"Have you—did you look down around the stable?"

The girl's eyes glared as they widened. She snatched Cynthia's arm and held it tightly.

"Who said anything about the stable? Who? It's a lie! Anybody who says they've seen me around the stable—"

The girl's startling, almost hysterical agitation took Cynthia aback. Why should the apparently casual mention of the stable cause her so much distress, unless she had some deep and awful feeling of guilt about it, so that even the suggestion that she might have dropped her pin there flung her into panic? Why, unless the stable hid some dark secret of her own? Something she so greatly feared might be uncovered that fear itself gave her away? And then, as the other's eyes shifted away from hers, Cynthia knew. Knew the whole revolting truth.

The girl had been making clandestine, furtive trips to the stable. Knowing what she would find waiting for her there. Going to *that,* to Jake, willingly, even eagerly. Stealing out in dead of night, heart already thumping with the excitement of her shame, drawn by some perverted, masochistic urge to destroy herself, fascinated by the defilement of both her young body and her soul, flinging herself into abasement, and finding in her final, shaken guilt the sustenance on which her sickness fed.

The pin had been lost on one of those degrading pilgrimages. Jake, finding it perhaps only minutes later, and already knowing to whom it belonged, had immediately hidden it, no doubt with the intention of selling it. Next day, however, fearing the pin might be picked up in or near the stable, fearing that its discovery could lead to some question which in turn would uncover the thin tissue of her deceptions, the girl had pretended to lose the pin in a very definite place—the dining hall.

Cynthia shrugged off the other's arm with unconcealed repugnance. They stood silently for a moment more before the girl said:

"You told me something when you did that. Something you've guessed about me, and something more about yourself. And, incidentally, whom to see about getting my pin back." And she walked away.

"Wait!" cried Cynthia, running after her. "What do you mean when you say that I've told you something about myself? Surely you don't think—"

"Never mind what I think," snapped the Johnson girl. "I'm going to the stable."

"And I'm going with you," Cynthia said breathlessly. She was full of fear, yet impelled by a strange fascination, an emotional compulsion she could not explain. She wanted to see the stable again, the scene of her horror, her degradation. Besides, she couldn't let this girl go on thinking that she, Cynthia, would willingly engage in adventures with the monsterlike Jake. She would have to explain...

Helen Johnson was running now. She ran into the stable with Cynthia just behind her. The Johnson girl paused, looked about angrily yet uncertainly in the dim half-light. The horses stamped uneasily. "Where's the pin?" she demanded.

"I found it in the hay—there, in Flame's stall. But *he* has it now." Cynthia gazed fearfully over her shoulder, but Jake was nowhere to be seen.

"He must have hidden it in his room." Helen Johnson, moving with the sureness that comes of familiarity, made her way through the stable-posts and stalls until she came to a rickety door festooned with harness gear and surmounted by a rusty horseshoe. She kicked it in violently, burst recklessly into Jake's sleeping quarters. Some of his clothes—ragged trousers and dirty shirts—hung from nails driven into the unpainted wall. A pint bottle of whiskey, half empty, stood on an old, scratched bureau. Bridles, bits, whips, hanging from the walls or carelessly flung in corners, gave the room the atmosphere of a stall rather than a bedroom. Everywhere there was evidence of the occupant, though he himself was not present. "Probably in the kitchen getting his dinner," muttered Helen. "That'll give me time to search."

She tore the room apart, questing into closets, drawers, boxes; she searched each shelf, tore apart the thin mattress on

Jake's bed. Unable to find the scatter-pin, she turned bitterly on Cynthia.

"You gave it to him," accused Helen, enraged. "You found it and you gave it to him! You knew it was mine. Why did you let him have it? Does he mean that much to you?"

"The trouble with you," Cynthia said coldly, "is that you're not really concerned about the pin. You're jealous. You think I'm trying to replace you in Jake's affections. True, he's had his sport with both of us. But there's a difference. I didn't volunteer for the game. He forced me to play it. So don't bother your pretty head about whether I'm trying to compete with you—"

"That's enough!" In a paroxysm of rage, Helen Johnson seized a buggy whip standing against the wall. "I'll teach you to say things like that! Why, you gave him my pin—you're no better than a common thief, a common—" She didn't finish. Instead, she swung the whip on Cynthia, striking her across the shoulders, the back and, as Cynthia collapsed to the floor under the fury of her blows, across her legs and upraised arms.

But Cynthia was a strong, athletic girl. This was one type of attack she could cope with. Though the first onslaught had taken her by surprise so that for a few moments she was too stunned to defend herself, she suddenly catapulted herself from the floor, plunging into Helen with all her force, and at the same time seizing the whip handle. The breath knocked out of her, Helen was unable to cling to the whip as Cynthia twisted with all her strength. With the whip in her hand, Cynthia felt all the humiliation and abasement of that day, first at the hands of Jake and now at the hands of Helen Johnson, welling up within her. Dispassionately, but vengefully, she plied the whip herself, driving back the cowering, screaming Helen. Suddenly Helen was on her knees, tears rolling down her face, begging for mercy. Cynthia, ashamed of herself for having used the whip, threw it to the floor.

"I'm sorry," sobbed Helen Johnson. "I lost my head. You were right to beat me. But you don't understand. He'll use that pin to blackmail me. He'll threaten to expose me to my family or the school, using the pin as proof that I'd been in the stable—here—alone with him. I've got to get it back. I've got to—"

Cynthia turned away, walked out of the stable, leaving the Johnson girl behind in Jake's room.

Her heart was pumping, her breast heaving with emotion and the effects of exertion. The fresh air struck her like a cleansing bath, but shame still seethed within her, and caused a blush on her cheek. And the shame was not entirely for having stooped to using the whip, she admitted to herself, but also for having derived an actual strange, deep satisfaction from belaboring Helen Johnson's soft shoulders with the stinging lash.

Cynthia ran back to her room, flung herself on the bed. She spent the night crying into her pillow.

It was a week after that when the stable burned. At about midnight someone raised a cry of fire, and everyone turned out to help. The horses were led out safely, but the stable could not be saved. During the excitement, and before he could be questioned, Jake disappeared. For a brief time there was a rumor that just before the blaze was discovered, a girl's screams had been heard coming from the stable; but it remained only a rumor.

A few days later the Johnson girl quit her courses and went home. Cynthia saw her leaving for the station. A scatter-pin sparkled brilliantly on the lapel of her suit, ransomed at what fearful cost Cynthia would not allow herself even to consider.

CHAPTER THREE

CYNTHIA stepped from the bus and looked about her. She was on Fifth Avenue in the Sixties, but, she surmised, about a block from her destination. She moved along briskly, a light breeze inquisitively blowing her spring coat away from her shoulders. Two men, passing by, nudged each other and gaped their appreciation, so she buttoned her coat again, although it was too warm that way.

She came to a corner, crossed, found that she had gone too far, and went back again. The first number she saw was lower than the one she wanted, but it was a professional building of some sort, so she went in. At least they could tell her what the right number was.

A tall young man, heavy, but giving the impression of slimness, was standing at a desk talking with another man who was studying something in a magazine.

"Well, look at it," he was saying. "It wouldn't matter if it was the best color-shot I ever took. When the public sees a thing printed off register like that, they think I—"

He caught sight of Cynthia and let the rest wait. He looked at her very carefully from where he stood, and then he came closer and looked at her some more. When he had looked at her for a long time he asked,

"Can I help you?"

"I'm trying to find a place called *House of Cimier*," Cynthia said, "but I'm not having much luck."

"Oh, sure. The beef trust. Right next door. Fools a lot of people because it actually faces on a crosstown street. But the entrance on Fifth gives them a swankier-sounding address that the chumps like. If you go up to the door and look around real careful-like, you'll see a little sign in letters about an inch high. That's the discreet way we advertise in this neighborhood ... Note, outside, the modest shingle which announces this as *Burton's Home for the Aged and Infirm*."

"Thank you so much," Cynthia said.

"Hey!" he called as she reached the door. "Tell those old biddies in there I have a slogan for them: 'Get slimmier with Cimier.' "

Cynthia shook her head. "Bad French," she objected.

"Right. 'Get immerslay mit Cimier'? Here we combine four great languages in four great words to make a universally intelligible whole. No, that's not quite it. No zing. Come back in five minutes and I'll have it. Or phone. Wire. Write. Send me a French postcard ... "

His voice trailed off behind her as the massive glass door pulled itself shut. "Barton's Home for the Aged," she noticed, was actually Barton's Studio of Photography. She turned to the Fifth Avenue entrance of the House of Cimier.

The foyer in which she found herself was abuzz with activity. Two dozen or more girls in street clothes stood about, some talking, some trying to get someone's attention, some merely eyeing the others appraisingly. With a quick, sinking feeling, Cynthia saw that several of them carried the telltale, narrow-folded newspaper of the job-hunter.

A girl with a bright, harrassed smile came up to her.

"Yes?"

"I was sent here by an employment agency," Cynthia said. "I certainly didn't expect this."

"Neither did we," replied the girl grimly. "The agency, you said? Well, I'm afraid—Oh, Miss Carter!" she called after a trim, tailored figure that was hurrying by.

"Make it fast, Meg," the woman said, stopping in full tilt, as though she were pausing for seconds only.

"Here's another one…"

"Well for heaven's sake, Meg!"

"…but *she's* from the agency!"

The woman turned her face full upon Cynthia for the first time. Shrewd, black eyes. A chin firm and determined. Brows that were dark and full and unplucked. Hair swept back in a neat, masculine cut.

"This way." She gestured with her head. Cynthia trotted after her as she strode through the cluster of girls and into a tiny office, kicked the door shut and perched on a corner of the desk.

"Don't bother to make yourself comfortable," she said without rudeness. "We won't be here long. I'm talking to you only because the agency sent you, and both you and they deserve an explanation of this mess. Yesterday I had to let a girl go, and called the agency for a replacement. Well, that little dreamboat evidently had a mean streak. Using the firm name, she phoned an ad into every paper in town, offering an outlandish salary! She knew damn well what would happen, and it did. On a day when we've got half a dozen classes to organize, the place is swarming with girls. Since they all ask for me by name, each one has to be questioned at least to the point where we know we're talking to a job applicant and not a potential customer. And there's always the chance—I'm not disparaging your qualifications, because I don't know what they are—that somewhere in that bunch marching in here today there may be the very girl I want. If she's turned away now, she won't be back again."

She stood up to lead Cynthia out.

"You can see what it is," she said. She waved a hand vaguely. "If you keep in touch with the agency, perhaps—in a few days… I don't know. I really don't know what to say."

Cynthia frowned doubtfully. Something had occurred to her, a possibility which Miss Carter must have overlooked—or perhaps considered and rejected. She decided to mention it anyway.

"Miss Carter ... "

The other swung around, her hand on the doorknob.

"I was just wondering why, if your staff isn't able to take care of this extra work, you don't hire one of those girls just for today, just to interview the others. I could do it myself, in fact, if I knew exactly what you were looking for."

Miss Carter smiled with a cynical amusement. But as she studied Cynthia's face, something she found there appeared to make her more thoughtful.

"It sounds like a trick idea out of a book on how to get a job," she said, "but I do believe you're serious."

She frowned a moment, then made a decision which she emphasized with a snap of her fingers.

"All right, I'll try it. Let me see ... If we had a poster to lead the girls into the waiting room across the hall—"

"I can do simple lettering. It wouldn't look professional—"

"Good. Make it fast, not fancy. I'll send somebody in to help you find the things you'll need. Use this office for the interviews." She went on to outline briefly what qualifications the applicants must have, and then left, promising over her shoulder to look in later and see how things were going.

Cynthia hung up her things and began looking for materials with which to do the poster. Several minutes later she was ready to begin the interviews. The first girl was called in. Trying to look very businesslike, Cynthia seated herself behind the desk and concentrated on concealing the trembling of the pen in her fingers.

"Name?" she said. "Age?"

By noon things were moving with a smoothness which, if not faultless, was at least sufficient to keep from a stranger's eyes the fact that anything unusual was going on at the House of Cimier. Girls arrived, were immediately notified that the wage offered in the newspaper ads was an error, and then either disappeared or lolled about with magazines or their papers until Cynthia called them. And an astonishing number, she found, were completely unfitted for the work they sought. They seemed to be impelled by some sort of nervous bravado, bolstered by a belief that if enough doors are tried, eventually one will be found open.

At about 12:30 there occurred a lull, and Cynthia found time for the sandwich and milk which she had sent out for earlier. She had been told to go to lunch whenever she wanted to, but she preferred to stay in the office, just in case. And it was quiet there, more relaxing than trying to battle the midday jams in the cafeterias. She felt content, now that the first pressure of the work had been eased. Even though the job was only for that day, she was happy. She had met a new situation and handled it well. There was a deep satisfaction in that.

She remembered her earlier musings on the possible character of Mr. J. Carter, and had to smile at her own naiveté. She should have remembered that this was New York, not Spragton. Home in Spragton you assumed that the head of a business must be a man. In New York it was simply assumed that to head a business one should be competent. As for the "Cimier" name, she was still uncertain. If there was a person by that name, he or she seemed to keep well in the background. Miss Carter was obviously in complete charge, and it might very well be that it was just a manufactured name.

Curiosity took over, and she picked up the phone book. She found House of Cimier quickly enough, but no individuals under that name. Of course, lots of people had unlisted phones ...

There came an announcing tap on the office door, and Miss Carter marched in with her curious, lengthy stride.

"Am I interrupting a call?" she asked. "I can come back later, if it's private."

"I wasn't phoning," Cynthia said. "I was just looking for 'Cimier' in the book."

"Oh, that. It's just a—but *child!* You didn't have to stay here during your lunch hour!"

Cynthia felt a twinge of annoyance at the use of the word "child." She was beginning to feel quite grown up, sitting behind that desk. Evidently the other sensed what was in her mind, for she went on,

"You've been doing wonderfully, Cynthia. I didn't have a chance to tell you before, but you've kept things going marvelously well. And even the way you handled that client who wandered in here by mistake—she told me she felt absolutely flattered to be mistaken for an instructor."

"A lucky accident," Cynthia laughed. "When I learned she'd been taking your home record course I saw a quick way out of a touchy situation, and I used it."

"Good. I like people around me who can think fast, and you seem able to. Now, is there anything you need? Is anything giving you trouble?"

Cynthia shook her head. "The only thing that bothers me," she said, "is the number of girls who haven't even the slightest qualification for the job. But I suppose that's due to the way the ad was worded."

The other smiled, as though at some private joke.

"I didn't expect any of them to qualify, Cynthia," she said quietly. "After all, you're not a complete idiot, and neither am I."

Before Cynthia could seek some further clarification of a statement which she found mystifying, a girl from the staff appeared.

"They're starting to arrive again," she announced. "Three just came in, one after the other."

Miss Carter started for the door.

"Just keep on as you have been doing," she said. "I probably won't see you this afternoon unless you run into trouble. Oh, and as for the name of the place—it's a little joke of mine. I'm afraid it's a bit coarse, and I probably wouldn't use it if I were starting out now. But that's the way I felt about some of my customers at the time. Try the French dictionary."

She nodded toward a shelf of directories and reference books and left.

Before she called in the first girl, Cynthia took a minute to leaf through the dictionary. *Ciergier… ciller… "Cimier,"* she read. *"Noun, masc. A buttock of beef."*

CHAPTER FOUR

I T was after five, and the last of the deluge of applicants had been heard and ushered out. Cynthia was cleaning up the odds and ends of debris, sorting notes which she had made, arranging cards in a system she had devised, when Miss Carter reappeared.

"Tough day?" she asked, dropping into a chair and casually hanging one knee over its arm.

"Not bad," Cynthia said. "But I wouldn't want to do it every day. I was just wondering what to do with these cards." She held up a rather bulky sheaf. "The agencies file them, I guess, but I don't know what you want done with them."

"Unsatisfactory, are they, Cynthia?"

"Impossible."

"As I expected. Well, file them in the wastebasket. Strange, isn't it, that among all those girls none fitted the job? Strange, but not surprising!" She smiled privately to herself, as before.

"Oh, but some of them *do* fit," Cynthia said. "This bunch." She passed over a much smaller handful of cards. "The better ones are on top," she explained. "There are two girls there who sound just right. One of them used to work for—"

"Just a minute." The woman held the cards in her hand without looking at them. "Do you mean to tell me you actually found some girls you think I should consider hiring? For a job *you* came after?"

"I guess I fit somewhere down in the last third of the pile," Cynthia said wryly. "I forgot to interview myself."

"Well, I'll be damned." Looking at the first three or four cards, Miss Carter rapidly scanned the information. "You really are precious! Tell me, are you for real, or did I just make you up out of my own head?"

Cynthia said nothing. She said nothing because she was not sure she understood what her employer was talking about.

The woman stood up and dropped the cards on the desk.

"Are you in a hurry?" she asked.

"No. I've nowhere to go except to dinner, and then either home or to a movie."

"You live alone?"

"Yes. I have a room down in the Village. I've been in New York only a few days."

"I see. Well, then suppose we make the Grand Tour of the House of Cimier. You haven't had a chance to look the place over. And I have a hundred questions to ask you. By the way, my name is Jan. To keep up a front, we call each other Miss this-or-that when there are clients about. But this is after hours. Understood?"

"I understand—Jan."

They walked down the hall, Jan keeping up a rapid-fire of questions and information.

"This used to be the old Furst mansion," she explained. "I'll tell you frankly that it's mortgaged, but I'm not worried about the mortgage. No wolves howl at my door these days, thank heaven. But I didn't have anywhere near enough cash to buy it outright, even at the ridiculously low price I paid. I just don't want you to think I'm wealthy or anything like it. This is a front which the business requires. I work for my living."

She emphasized the remark with a momentary silence, as though to be sure her words sank in.

"This place was a real white elephant," she went on. "Furst built it as a home for his wife and two children after all three of them had been stricken with polio. That explains the swimming pool which takes up half the basement, the self-service elevators, and a lot of other things which make the place impractical for the average buyer and which made it so nearly perfect for me."

They stopped before a doorway which set off the offices and lounges from the rest of the rooms.

"We are about to enter," said Jan, "the Decontamination Center. Beyond this door are the dressing rooms. No one goes through the dressing rooms and into the rest of the building in street clothes. That includes me. If a client is chasing around in a chic outfit made up of a towel and a smile, she's entitled to freedom from the sort of discomfort most people feel at finding themselves half-dressed in front of someone fully dressed. You know that defenseless feeling? So a playsuit is practically formal from here on. And, reversing the procedure, no one comes out of this door in anything that couldn't be worn on the subway. Clear?"

Cynthia nodded.

"Now," Jan continued, "if you aren't tired, I'd like to see how you are in the gym. That's upstairs, on the next floor."

They entered a large room fitted out with dressing cubicles, lockers, and showers. From a huge cupboard Jan selected a green, two-piece outfit for Cynthia, then went to a locker evidently her own and laid out another suit for herself. Without bothering to use a dressing closet, she slipped out of her jacket and tossed it carelessly on a table.

"You'll find new sneakers in that chest," she said, motioning with that toss of her head which was becoming familiar. "Wool socks on the right." She unbuttoned her blouse, then unzipped her skirt and stepped out of it. A fingernail snagged her stocking, and she bent over to examine the damage, stretching her long leg out sideways.

"Damn!" she exclaimed. "Well, it's not too bad."

She looked up and found Cynthia staring at her.

"Is something the matter?" she asked.

Cynthia shook her head negatively. She had not made a move toward changing her own clothes, but was watching the other's compact narrow-hipped body with a kind of troubled fascination.

"I didn't mean to be rude," she said. "It's just that the way you stood then reminded me of something. Something I thought I had forgotten. But I'm afraid it wouldn't sound the way I mean it if I tried to explain."

Jan laughed, a deep bubble of friendliness seeming to rise and break in her throat.

"Tell me," she urged. "I can't stand secrets. And if I'm insulted, I shall of course scratch out your lovely eyes."

"Well," Cynthia said, "there was a farm boy who lived near a summer camp I attended. He had captured a hawk, and he was trying to train it to hunt. He'd gotten hold of some books on falconry, and he seemed to know all the terms, even if he wasn't having much luck when it came to actual training. He even had a word to describe what a bird does when it puts a leg out to one side and stretches its wing over it. They call it 'mantling.' I remembered it, because it always looked like a ballet step to me." She looked distressed. "I'm afraid you're disappointed. There wasn't any point to it, was there?"

Jan laughed again, shortly. She thrust her nylon-clad leg out again and stretched her fingers down along it, cocking her head in a birdlike manner.

"A hawk?" she mused. "Well, perhaps. I've hardly the profile, but heaven knows I've the instinct. But you," she said suddenly, "aren't changing. If you want privacy, take one of the dressing closets."

"It isn't that at all," Cynthia protested. "I was daydreaming." She began to undress quickly.

"I hope he was a nice boy," Jan said abruptly. "That boy with the hawk."

She had unfastened her brassiere, and she was slowly massaging herself, as though her flesh had been too strictly confined.

"I didn't know much about him. He was just the boy on the farm where we got our eggs."

"Oh." Jan's glance slipped sideways at Cynthia, who was struggling with her slip. "I thought it was one of the important ones. Here, let help you."

Her slender, warm fingers slid over Cynthia's golden skin as she helped her peel out of the garment, resting perhaps an infinitesimally longer instant than necessary on the girl's shoulders.

"There haven't been any important ones," Cynthia said from beneath the folds of cloth which muffled her voice.

"I see." Jan laid the slip out carefully and pushed her own panties down over sleek hips.

Why, Cynthia wondered, did women seem so much more naked in just stocking and shoes? There was more—provocation, was probably the word—in that state of nudity. She found it impossible to keep her eyes elsewhere, and Jan seemed to know that Cynthia's attention was on her body. There was a quality of awareness underlying everything she did. Every move seemed studied, premeditated, as though she were deliberately displaying herself to the best advantage.

It became very quiet in the dressing room. So quiet that the snap of metal hooks as Jan unfastened her garter belt sounded unnaturally loud, became unnaturally important.

"Does everyone leave at five?" Cynthia asked in an effort to break that seemingly significant silence.

Jan glanced at her watch as she unstrapped it.

"Yes. We're quite alone now. The cleaning women come in early in the morning. Occasionally I'm here in the evening with a client who, for one reason or another, wants private attention, but that doesn't happen often. After five you could commit a murder here without fear of interruption—a great temptation, with some of the people we have to deal with."

She finished the change into her gym outfit and lolled back against the wall, hands behind her, as she watched Cynthia.

"Lucky thing that halter is adjustable," she observed. "Old Mom Nature was wonderfully generous with you, wasn't she? Here, let me help."

"I can manage," Cynthia said. She altered the strap and fumbled with the plastic fastener.

Moments later they were on their way to the elevator. As they passed each room, Jan tossed off a cryptic listing of its contents and their purpose.

"Steam boxes and sun lamps in here. Massage room on our left. All hair-dressing, facials, electrolysis—things like that—are done in the front of the building. On the third floor, accessible by way of the front elevator, there are classrooms where we teach makeup, clothes selection and so on. But we put a lot of emphasis on body conditioning, so the gym is really the big deal."

The elevator carried them smoothly to the second floor, and they stepped directly into the gymnasium.

"The gym takes up the entire floor," Jan explained, "with the exception of two small rooms. One of those is for storage of equipment. The other is for those women who want privacy while they are having their bottoms jiggled by an electric belt or are trying to hang onto a mechanical horse."

Cynthia looked about the large, open room with surprise. Flying rings and climbing-ropes hung from the ceiling. There were pull-weights along one wall, balance bars along two others. Scattered about were rowing machines, friction bicycles, vaulting horses, parallel bars, and a host of other paraphernalia.

"It's certainly very complete," she said.

"Even to a trampoline which no one uses," Jan pointed out. "I got it all in a package from a boys' school that failed. Well, shall we get started? I've got a few basic setting-up exercises that everyone begins with and is supposed to continue every day. Just watch me and follow."

Facing each other, the two went through a simple routine of torso-twisting and back-stretching, leg bends and toe-touching.

"That's for beginners," Jan said, stopping. "Now we'll get on to some more advanced things."

She demonstrated a dozen or more exercises which became progressively more difficult. Cynthia followed easily, her body responsive to every demand.

"That's about as far as most of our clients ever get," Jan said, springing lightly to her feet as she came out of a forward roll. "However, it doesn't hurt if you're able to take a few hardy souls further. Can you use the rings? The parallel bars?"

For answer, Cynthia illustrated by catching the two iron rings and flinging herself into space with a short run. She swung forward and thrust her legs straight upward as she reached the peak of the arc. Head downward, she rode back, the loose material of her gym pants fluttering. Turning completely over at the top of the back-swing, she used her body's weight to build up her forward motion.

"Hey!" she heard Jan call mildly. "Take it easy up there!"

Higher and higher she swung, until it seemed that any increase in momentum must bring her to the very ceiling. Then, carefully gauging the height of the rings at their closest position to the floor, she thrust her feet through them and hung by her heels. As she had judged, she was barely able to brush the floor with her fingertips. Then the floor was receding again. She was flying up and up, arching her back to take advantage of the highest point of the pendulum swing.

Her badly fastened halter chose that moment to come undone and flutter gaily into space.

She saw Jan side-step and capture it as it dropped. Bare to the waist, she swung through the forward arc, then pulled herself upward and grasped the ropes, disengaging her feet. She had to swing back once more, hanging by her hands, breasts pulled taut by the strain, before she could drop from the rings with a short, forward run. Jan was at her side at once.

"You had me frightened to death," she exclaimed, holding the halter for Cynthia to slip into. "Please, *please,* use the mats if you're going aloft like that."

Flushed, whether from her exertions or from embarrassment would have been difficult to say, Cynthia docilely allowed Jan to fasten the strap.

"I won't say 'I told you so,' " Jan Carter said with a mischievously malicious purr in her voice, "but these dratted things are tricky until you're used to them. Here, wait a minute. Good heavens, Cynthia, you're coming undone all over!"

Before Cynthia realized what her intention was, the woman had dropped to one knee before her and was retying a lace which had come loose.

Cynthia looked down at the top of Jan's bowed head as she bent over her self-imposed task. For the most fleeting fraction of a second she had an impulse to put out her hand and touch the tousled hair which brushed lightly against her thigh. Then the impulse faded, and Jan was on her feet again.

But something of what Cynthia had felt must have echoed in her eyes, for, as their glances met, a strangeness crept into the exchange. It was as though a question, unspoken, and by one not understood, lay between them.

Jan suddenly gave Cynthia a sisterly pat on the bottom.

"Beat you up the ropes to the rafters," she challenged.

Together they raced to two three-inch ropes, leaped, and hauled themselves upward, hand over hand. Jan reached the top first, wound her leg securely about the rope and rested, apparently as comfortably as in an easy chair. A moment later Cynthia supported herself similarly. They hung there, catching their breath, swaying slightly to and fro.

"Not bad for an old woman of twenty-five," Jan said approvingly of herself. "By the way, how old are you, Cynthia?"

"Nineteen. But I feel like a very aged and creaky monkey just now."

"I imagine we'd both appear rather simian to a stranger," Jan said. She scratched herself in an absorbed apelike burlesque. "Charm and poise await you at the House of Simians," she declaimed. "Observe the charming poise of the prime primate." She grimaced frightfully. "I make a lousy boss," she concluded thoughtfully. "How can I expect the help to respect me if I make an ass—pardon, I'm a monkey, aren't I?—a monkey, then, of myself in front of them?"

Cynthia protested. "It's after five o'clock," she reminded. "What Jan does has nothing to do with what Miss Carter does. In fact, I don't even think it's any of Miss Carter's business."

"Oh, that awful Miss Carter! I hear she dyes her hair and has an idiot love-child in St. Louis."

"Did you notice that her dentures don't fit?" Cynthia offered. "She's too cheap to get good ones."

"She got them second-hand at a church raffle," Jan confided. "She buys all her clothes at rummage sales."

"She picks her nose when she thinks people aren't looking."

"They say she used to be in a circus cooch-show until she went on the drink. She used to bathe in those days."

"Then she went in the side-show and bit the heads off chickens—"

"—but it bothered her post-nasal drip—"

"—so she took to selling heroin—"

"—until she developed a six-cap habit herself."

"She went down and down and down—"

"—until she was lower than a policeman, even."

"Then she stole the egg-money from her poor, blind old mother's sugar bowl—"

"—and opened a charm-school."

"A bad end, a bad end," Cynthia said gloomily.

They shook their heads over the unfortunate creature.

"I'm going to spoil it," Cynthia said suddenly. "I'm going to giggle."

They laughed together, swaying back and forth in what must have seemed an alarming fashion, had anyone been there to observe them. Then, they slid swiftly down the ropes.

"I like you," Jan Carter said as they recrossed the floor. "You're fun. But that's no reason to hire anyone. I'm running a business, and from a business viewpoint, I think you'll do. I'll give you a beginner's class to start with. Posture, general limbering up. Your biggest problem will be holding down the hell-for-leather gals who try to kill themselves the first few days, seeing that they don't rattle their kidneys loose on the vibrator belt and things like that. And, incidentally, don't kill *yourself* the first few days."

She motioned Cynthia into the elevator, and they descended.

"Make it a point to get a rub-down every night, at least at first. An instructor crippled up with stiff muscles wouldn't inspire much confidence, I'm afraid. So let's start off right. The rubbing tables are in here, you remember."

Heading Cynthia into the room, she snapped on a light and gestured to one of the padded tables.

"Take off your clothes and climb up on there," she said. She turned to a wall cabinet and began rattling through bottles. Over her shoulder she added, "I suppose you can find a towel or sheet if you're modest."

"I'm not," Cynthia said.

That was not the truth, and she knew it. She had been acutely disturbed when she and Jan were changing their clothes, horribly mortified at the incident of the renegade halter. But she was instinctively aware that her modesty was something other than natural. It was, she felt, an over-reaction to what Jake had done to her that night in the stable, a psychic scar which must somehow be healed.

Her lips firmed, and she stripped with deliberate, quick efficiency. Then she stretched out, face down, on the table and waited.

"This is going to feel cold," Jan said warningly.

Cynthia's back muscles tensed as the rubbing alcohol dribbled over her skin. Instantly Jan's palm was in quick pursuit, spreading the coolness evenly over the entire upper part of her back.

"I wish I could give you all of this evening," Jan said as she gently began to knead Cynthia's shoulders. "There are dozens of things we ought to discuss before you take a class. But I'm tied up for dinner—you're tightening up, Cynthia; try to relax—and the rest of the evening as well. I'll give you some of our literature, though, and you can bone up on that tonight."

Her fingers pressed along Cynthia's spine and followed its arching curve downward in long, firm sweeps. Then she began working her hands with a quick and catlike treading motion, too firm to be gentle, yet too gentle to be painful. Cynthia's skin began to glow warmly. A feeling of laziness, almost drowsiness, crept through her. Muscles which had quickened to resistance at the first touch of alien fingers, resisted no longer, gave themselves up to that persistent manipulation and became pliantly yielding. By degrees that were imperceptible the pressure was increased, until Cynthia realized that she was being massaged with a vigor that should have been uncomfortable, but somehow wasn't.

Jan's hand brushed quickly over the swell of her hips and rested quietly on the back of her thigh.

"You remind me of a young pony," Jan said. "That pert little croup should be switching a tail."

She began massaging Cynthia's legs, working slowly down over her calves to her heels. Cynthia grunted softly, implying a contentment which she did not quite feel.

Why, she was drowsily wondering. Why do I find myself disturbed by her? Is it a simple, normal resistance to being touched so intimately? Would it be different if we weren't almost strangers? Or if we were *really* strangers, if I were just another client, for instance? Or is it because I know we're alone here, because I'm uneasy now when I'm alone with anyone?

She turned the problem over and over in her mind, like a strange coin to be examined, while Jan's competent hands worked just behind her knees, loosening the stiffened muscles extending down from her thighs. There was a wonderful physical relief in the touch of those hands, but she found her mind becoming more and more distressed. With a firm determination to master herself, to subdue that mental disquiet, Cynthia moved her legs, stiffening them so as to offer more resistance to Jan's hands—and at that instant the massaging stopped.

"You're cooked brown on this side," Jan said lightly. "Be an obliging little fish and flop over in the pan."

"I feel wonderful right now," Cynthia hesitated.

"Fine. But did you ever have a charlie horse in the front of your thigh? I did. No fun."

From somewhere she produced a towel and tossed it casually over the lower part of Cynthia's body. Then, rapidly, she massaged first her arms and finally her legs. But, brief as that contact was, it left Cynthia's nerves screaming. There was, she discovered, some vast and important difference between lying face down, so that she could not see what was happening, and actually watching her body being handled. It was as though she could accept the outrage—for outrage it was to her scarred mind—of her body through but one sense at a time. She could be touched if she did not have to see herself touched. She could undress before another woman, but shrank from any personal contact then—even if it were so simple a matter as having a recalcitrant halter strap secured.

"Have you ever been done in oil?" Jan was asking.

It seemed like an odd question.

"No," she said. "We had a sketching class, and a friend of mine tried a water-color of me once—"

"You bit!" Jan said accusingly. "You're slowing down." She poured a thimbleful of massage oil into her palm and waved the bottle label in front of Cynthia's eyes. "Just for that you don't get to hear what was found in that Carter person's dirty laundry last week. Over again, please. Once over lightly on your back."

Cynthia obediently turned and offered her back.

"A man's shirt with six sleeves," she hazarded.

"Ah, but what *color?*" Jan exclaimed. "Baby pink, with green stripes. Now I ask you, what sort of man would wear a thing like that? Obviously he's a boor and a bounder."

Her hands slid sleekly over Cynthia's oiled skin, grasping little handfuls of slippery flesh and immediately losing them. As the relaxed swells of muscle slipped elusively away from the pressure of Jan's fingers, they tended to draw together, to firm themselves without actually tensing. In effect it was as though Jan, having taken her body, having overcome its resistance and established a kind of dominance over it, now, subtly relinquished her possession and returned that body to Cynthia stimulated and glowing with a sense of well-being. More quickly than Cynthia expected, Jan finished and briskly toweled off the excess oil.

"Run along and start your shower," Jan said. "You'll find a cap somewhere. I'll be with you in a minute."

"But if I'm to be treated like a delicate orchid," Cynthia suggested, "what about your own rub-down? I know I couldn't do it as well as you—"

"I'll take a rain-check. The gym is everyday routine for me, so it's not important. And I've got to hurry to keep my appointments. But thanks, anyway."

Cynthia rolled off the table, picked up her gym suit and trotted to the shower. Jan followed some time later, and while she was still bathing, Cynthia finished and dressed. Afterward she roamed out into the hall, acquainting herself with the various rooms and what they contained. A shrill whistle finally summoned her.

"Mind being whistled at?" Jan grinned. "I wasn't sure where you were."

"When I was little," Cynthia remembered, "I was always envious of the boys who could whistle through their fingers like that."

"It's easy," Jan told her. "You just take two fingers and—" She finished with an ear-splitting blast.

"It's no use trying to teach me," Cynthia said. "I gave up long ago."

They went back through the hall, Jan turning out lights as she went. At the office where Cynthia had spent that day, Jan stopped and picked up the cards which she had earlier dropped on the desk.

"We won't be needing these," she said. "The opening has been filled."

She dropped them into the wastebasket.

"Seems like a stupid waste of your time and theirs, doesn't it? Well, Cynthia, it wasn't your fault or mine, so there's no use being upset over it."

The door-latch clicked emphatically as they went out onto the street.

"Can I drive you somewhere?" Jan asked. "My car is around the corner."

"Thanks, but after being in all day, I think I'll walk a few blocks." Cynthia shifted the books and looseleafs Jan had given her.

"Tomorrow, then. And Cynthia—"

"Yes?"

"Relax. You seem to be all bound up, like a spring that's too tight. Whatever is chewing at you can't be worth it. If it's anxiety about the job, forget it. You'll get along all right."

"I'll try to unwind," Cynthia promised. "Good night."

They separated, and Cynthia started down the avenue. As she passed Barton's Studio she glanced in. The tall, young man to whom she had spoken that morning was seated at a desk, working at something. He looked up in time to see her, recognized her, and wigwagged an exuberant greeting. Cynthia raised two fingers in a more restrained reply and walked on. She wondered about him briefly, and without much curiosity. Before she had gone half a block she had forgotten him completely.

CHAPTER FIVE

FIFTEEN women lay on their backs in various unlikely attitudes. Cynthia stood before them and called directions in a rhythmic cadence.

"Right leg up—over—stretch—and back. Left leg up—over—"

The ringing of the wall-phone broke in on her attention.

"All together, now," she said. "Let's hear it."

"—and back," the women chorused. "Right leg up—"

She stepped to the phone and lifted the receiver. It was one of the girls from the business office. The one called Meg.

"—over—stretch—and back," fifteen voices droned.

"You'll have to speak louder," Cynthia said into the mouthpiece. "It's noisy up here."

Something about government employment forms to fill out.

"I'll meet you in no-man's-land," Meg said.

That was, Cynthia knew, a tiny room off the dressing room, neutral ground set aside by mutual agreement for the transaction of small affairs of business between the office force and those who worked on the "undressed" side of the building.

Cynthia formed her class in a circle, gave them a medicine ball to pass around, and, after asking another instructor to keep an eye on things, skipped down one flight without bothering to use the elevator. Meg was waiting for her, a sheaf of papers in her hand.

"Social security, state and federal tax claims, and so on and so forth," she explained, handing Cynthia a pen.

Cynthia sat down and began filling in the blanks.

"Like the job?" Meg asked, seating herself and leafing idly through a copy of *Vogue*.

"How do you spell—oh, I remember," Cynthia said absently. "The job? Oh, wonderful. I like it very much."

Meg's eyes were naturally large and far apart. Mascara and eye-shadow exaggerated their size. She flickered a side-long glance at Cynthia and said,

"You stayed late last night, didn't you?"

"Hmm? Oh yes. Ja—Miss Carter wanted to talk to me, of course. And then we spent some time in the gym."

"That must have taken quite a while." Meg flipped the magazine pages with an air of ennui.

"Quite a while, yes," Cynthia agreed, frowning over an obscure paragraph of governmental gobbledegook. "I hardly noticed, because I was really having fun. Miss Carter isn't exactly what you'd expect an employer to be like."

"That sounds as though it weren't all strictly business."

"I guess it wouldn't have appeared like the usual business interview," Cynthia said. "She's a pretty warm and human person."

"I'm sure *you* found her so."

The tone was so chilling that Cynthia looked up in quick surprise. Meg tossed her magazine aside and jumped up with an air of impatience.

"I suppose if you're going to dawdle over those papes all day, I might as well go back and get some work done," she said. "Just leave them when you're through. I'll pick them up later."

She went out, leaving Cynthia looking after her in complete bewilderment.

It was depressing, as well as baffling, to be snapped at like that, and Cynthia spent several minutes in trying to determine what she had done or said to precipitate such a reaction. There had been, she now realized, an odd undercurrent running throughout their conversation. Meg had been probing for something, some information the significance of which Cynthia did not grasp. There had been resentment in her questioning, and a catty implication of some strange sort.

What *had* she been trying to learn? Cynthia wondered. And, at what unspoken conclusion had she arrived, to be so much annoyed? It would have been more understandable, to some extent, if Meg and she had been doing the same sort of work. There would have been the explanation of natural rivalry in that case, a normal resentment toward a newcomer. But Meg was an office worker, as much Jan's secretary as anything else, and there was no apparent reason why a new girl in the gym should upset her.

As completely in the dark as before, Cynthia finished the forms and started back to her class.

The door of the massage room, as she passed it, opened, and one of the two operators—a heavy, placid-eyed woman with muscular, freckled arms and a reddish fuzz on her upper lip—came out on some errand. Looking past her, Cynthia was somewhat startled to find that the second masseur was a man. Beefy and bored, he stood at a table on which a rather artificially pretty woman of thirty-five was lying, a piece of sheeting over her hips. His thick fingers grabbed and pulled, grabbed and pulled, and little sighs that were half squeals breathed from the woman's lips.

"Oh, Arthur," Cynthia heard her say, "you're being much too easy on me today."

Happening to look up, he saw Cynthia, and one eyelid dropped heavily, lizardlike, in a cold wink of complicity. Nodding contemptuously toward the woman who lay before him, he raised his arms powerfully and began a vigorous pummelling. The white, rounded body writhed and wriggled, twisting in a fashion that was almost openly sensual. Under the loud, smacking sound of those large hands could be heard the woman's happy, hurt voice.

"Oooh … oooh … *oooh!*"

The door closed.

There were a great many enigmas, Cynthia began to realize, under the dignified mansard roof of the quiet brownstone on Fifth Avenue.

Lunchtime found Cynthia in a cafeteria on Lexington. It was crowded, and as she stood with her tray she at first saw no place to sit. Then she understood that a certain wave was intended to attract her attention. It was the photographer again, and he was indicating that he had saved her a place at his table.

From what little she knew of him, he seemed rather odd, and she was not at all sure that she wanted to encourage their acquaintanceship. But, since she obviously had no table, it would have been a direct snub to refuse his offer—and she had, as yet, no reason to actively dislike him. She carried her tray over and set it down rather warily.

"I followed you here," he said with immediate frankness. "I chased you for two blocks, but I hadn't quite caught up when you turned in here. So I spotted a table for us. And now, if you'll excuse me, I'll get something to eat."

He strode to the counter and was back in a few minutes with a laden tray. He was, Cynthia observed, one of those people who, without demanding it, are served at once.

"I saw you going into the House of Horrors this morning," he said as he settled down. "You don't look as though you need their services, so I'm assuming you work there."

"As of today," Cynthia said.

"Like it? Good boss?"

"Yes—to both questions."

"Good. By the way, I don't know your name. Mine hangs over my door, if you've noticed. The full job is William Ridgefield Barton, and I would rather be called Bill. You're not a native New Yorker, are you?"

"I'm Cynthia Bennett, and I'm from Spragton, Pennsylvania."

Bill Barton tested his coffee and found it too hot.

"Spragton," he observed, "is a good place to be from. A long way from. I spent three weeks between trains there, one rainy afternoon."

"You're plagiarizing from Dorothy Parker."

"That's the way it is. Every time I say something clever, that Parker girl said it first. They blame everything on her, including original sin."

"Besides, Spragton is a real up-and-coming place. They have a real live elephant at the zoo. The morning paper ran a big campaign to buy her, and I own fifty cents' worth. Do *you* own fifty cents' worth of an elephant?"

"No," he admitted. "I was an underprivileged child. But I once had seventeen thousand and fifty-four points toward a Shetland pony. If I hadn't run out of relatives to sell flower seeds to, I'd have made it. As it was, the company sent me some writing paper and a certificate of merit."

"Everybody tells sad stories about his childhood," Cynthia complained. "Didn't *anybody* have any fun?"

"I'm making up for it now," Bill said. "I have fun every day, all day long. It has something to do with being bull-headed enough to believe that you yourself know what's best for you. I never take advice—I just pass it on to other people."

He tried his coffee again, and began sipping it.

"Cynthia Bennett," he mused. "Did anyone ever call you Cyn?"

"Not regularly, as I remember. Nicknames never stuck to me."

"Well, tell the old crow who runs that place that I have an advertising campaign mapped out for her. We'll put your picture all over town, with the name 'Cyn Bennett' under it. And the copy will simply run, 'We'll Make You Pretty As Cyn.' "

"She's not an old crow," Cynthia said. "She's very lovely. No, not lovely. She's ... "

"Handsome," Bill supplied. "I've seen her. She walks the street like some half-tamed animal on an invisible leash. I wonder what would happen if she broke loose?"

"Oh, she'd eat half a dozen children right in the middle of their sad childhood, and then curl up somewhere and go to sleep purring. Do you always characterize people so oddly? It must be rather frightening to feel yourself to be surrounded by a world of escaped circus animals and things like that."

"I wasn't analyzing her character, I was passing along an impression. It's probably a hangover from a picture book I did— juxtapositions of people and animals who looked alike or were doing the same things."

"Tell me about your work," Cynthia said. "Do you specialize in things like that?"

"No. Actually, I do almost anything that comes along. It started in college, when I found out that people would buy prints of the shots I took for the college paper. After college I began kidnapping babies—"

"What!"

"Riding around and trying to make photographic appointments at houses where I saw children playing," he explained with a grin. "You know: 'We Shoot Your Child In The Privacy Of Your Home.' Then I did weddings, banquets, company dances, minstrel shows, dance recitals, summer theatres, commercial work. Finally I opened a small studio upstate and began picking up night-club photo concessions until I had a string of them. About a year ago I sold out, came to New York, and—well, here I am. Right now I do a lot of advertising work and play around with a couple of new picture books. I guess that's the whole sordid story."

"It sounds as though you've kept busy," Cynthia said. "Do you know, this is the first job I ever had?"

"That so? How'd you happen to hit it?"

"Through an agency, by a sort of fluke. I'd really hoped to get into modeling, but I was willing to try anything."

"Modeling?" He sighed and slowly buttered a roll. "Why the devil do they all want to be models? It's supposed to be glamorous, I guess. And they all make the same mistake—try to become smart, sophisticated types overnight."

Cynthia said nothing. It seemed like a good time to listen.

"If you saw some of the girls I try to work with," he went on, "you'd know why my hair is graying in my late twenties. Young pups, who would look cute in their own floppity way, come in looking as though they were playing dress-up in their mothers' naughtiest party clothes. They stand in any of five ungraceful attitudes, and the shift from one position to another is like the working of a machine. God alone knows what they really look like, because they enamel haughty, under-fed masks over their faces. And they're bored, these little squirts. So bored and blasé, that sometimes I think they've fallen asleep. Once in a while I find one who is willing to scrub her face and act natural, but most of them simply irritate me to a point where I'd like to turn them over my knee and paddle the cheeks they don't paint. Or—good lord, I wonder—*do* they?"

Cynthia blushed and inwardly squirmed, as she always did when people made references even remotely sexual. Bill's eyes studied her calmly as he took out cigarets.

"Do you know how I get models for a lot of my work? I scout the high schools and the coke joints. When I find a girl who is right, I insist on meeting her ma, so that there's no question about things being on the up-and-up. Or, one day, I find myself sitting in a cafeteria with a girl who blushes and has a milk mustache."

Realizing that the reference was to herself, Cynthia took a paper napkin and patted her lips.

"I'm doing a catalogue right now," Bill said. "It's for a good line of clothes, very clever, and very—how you all-same say in 'Melican?—trig. The market is rural, and the appeal is to the farm girl who wants to look smart. This girl has no hayseed in her ears, but we recognize the fact that anything too sophisticated might scare off her parents. I need wholesome-looking models who also have a certain flair, an élan which barely hints of things like formal dances, evenings at the theatre, and dinner at places where the menu is in French. Do you want to try it?"

"*Do* I!" Cynthia exclaimed. "But—when? I work all day."

"So we'll make it in the evening. This evening, if you say so. Anytime after five."

Her attention brought to the subject of time, Cynthia found that she was overstaying her lunch hour.

"Golly," she said, "I'll have to rush. No, let me have my check. Thank you."

"I'll walk back with you," Bill said.

Several minutes later they were standing in front of Bill's studio, confirming their appointment. Bill gave her a few last-minute instructions.

"If you color your nails," he said, "we'll only have to remove it. And, whatever you do, don't have your hair done, or we can't work for two days."

"All right, Bill."

At that moment a voice spoke a greeting. It was Meg, returning from her own lunch, who had passed by just in time to hear Cynthia speak Bill's name. She smiled in a pleasant fashion, made some remark about the weather, and, after nodding at Bill, went jauntily on.

"That's strange," Cynthia mused. "She almost took my head off this morning. Well, I'll see you after five, then."

She went back to her work in a much better frame of mind than she had left. By sheer luck, she felt, she had fallen first into a permanent job she liked, and then into a chance to do some modeling—and in each case the persons involved seemed to be human beings. Now Meg had gotten over her huff, whatever its cause may have been. Things looked far better than she could have hoped for, a few short days ago.

Cynthia hummed softly as she passed Jan's office and collected a bonus in the shape of another friendly smile. On her horizon there were no clouds.

Somewhere, and slowly, the storm gathered unseen.

CHAPTER SIX

"BUT Cynthia," Jan objected, a quizzical half-frown clouding her face, "I rather expected that we'd get together this evening and go over things. There are so many rough edges to smooth out—and we didn't have time today, busy as we all were."

"I'm sorry," Cynthia said in a crestfallen manner. "It didn't occur to me that you might be planning anything like that. I made the appointment without thinking."

The two were in Jan's office. It was shortly after five, and the building was rapidly being emptied of both clients and staff. Cynthia had already showered and was dressed for the street.

"It's not your fault. It's mine for assuming that your evenings weren't tied up," Jan said.

"But it won't be for the entire evening," Cynthia explained. "He said just an hour or so."

"And you're going to model—clothes?"

"Yes, for a catalogue."

"I suppose I could catch up on some things here and wait for you."

"I'll break the appointment," Cynthia said suddenly, but without much enthusiasm.

"No, don't do that. I can meet you afterward. Good night, Mrs. Cartwright. Good night, Evelyn," she said toward the open door.

"If there's nothing awfully important for you to do here," Cynthia suggested, "I do wish you could come with me. Oh I know I shouldn't ask you to give me your time for a thing like this, but—I'm shaky. I don't know the first thing about what I'm to do, and I'm sure I'll make a mess of things and do it all wrong."

"Does Mr. Barton have assistants working at night too?"

"I don't know. I didn't ask."

"And you have just met him in the last two days? Perhaps I should go along—unless I'd be in the way."

"I do wish you would," Cynthia repeated, more earnestly now as she realized that there was a possibility of finding herself alone with Bill Barton.

Meg appeared at the door with a couple of manila envelopes.

"May I come in?" she asked. "These need filing."

"Still here, Meg?" Jan said casually. "Well, if you're going to be a few more minutes, Cynthia and I can run along and let you lock up."

Meg bit her lip and nodded, expressionless. But, had Cynthia turned as she and Jan left, she would have discovered the girl looking after them, her face a study of mixed emotions, of which speculation, anger, and disappointment were perhaps the most easily read.

Bill Barton's office door was open, and he was marking out proofs for correction when they entered.

"I brought a chaperone," Cynthia said with an attempt at lightness. She murmured introductions.

Glances touched like epées, warily.

"I'm glad you brought someone," said Bill. "There are things like model release forms to sign, and you ought to have someone look them over, if you're not familiar with them."

He led the way back to the actual working part of the studio. This was a large, high-ceilinged room which reminded Cynthia of a car barn or an armory in its first impression of bare func-tionalism. Then she saw that it was broken up into compact sec-tions, each an identifying slice from a familiar whole. There was a tiny strip of sandy beach with various nautical props standing ready, and next to it was a spot which could have been part of a lawn or a golf course. Here was a kitchen, there two sides of a living room, and next a set which could have been a hospital ward or an operating room. There were three sectional booths which could have come from almost any bar or tea room—or might have been pews in a church. There was the door and one window of a small house, but the picture window had been doing double duty, for it was presently the plate-glass front of a bakery store. The settings seemed endless, filled with unexpected variations. In addition, the adaptability of props and settings made the possible combinations almost without limit.

"It's amazing," Cynthia marveled. "I always thought, when I looked at a picture, that I was seeing—well, what my eyes told me."

"That's what you're supposed to think," Bill grinned. He snapped on a few lights, and a corner of a flagged terrace came into being. A pleasant nook with a barbecue fireplace and summer furniture waiting for the arrival of some smart, suburban party.

"Wonderful! I can even hear the mosquitos," Jan applauded.

"That's a carbon light. But if insects bother you … "

He switched off that bank of lights and turned on others. Moving a few steps, they found themselves snugly ensconced in a rugged ski lodge, or cabin. Crossed snow shoes hung ready on the chinked-log walls. The mounted head of a caribou peered fiercely out of the upper shadows. Rough Indian blankets were scattered here and there. Through one small and frosted window a chill blue reflection sparkled off drifted snow on the sill and shimmered through a hanging pattern of icicles.

"Brrr!" Cynthia exclaimed. "I'm not dressed for it."

Bill flicked another switch, and what had been the terrace fireplace now became the lighted fireplace of the cabin, throwing a warm and hearty glow over all.

"I don't believe it," Cynthia said. "It's magic."

Wiping away the illusion with a snapping of switches, Bill became more businesslike.

"I've saved four outfits for you," he said. "You'll find them in the dressing-room over there. They'll almost fit, but where they need to be neatened up, Miss Carter can help out with clothes pins."

"You mean safety pins, don't you?"

"Clothes pins. The hinged kind, with springs."

He shooed her toward the dressing room. Jan followed and sat down on a bench, watching as Cynthia shed her outer clothing.

"What do you think of him?" Cynthia asked, hanging up her blouse and unfastening her skirt.

Jan hesitated for a long, unsure moment. Then she forced a rather unsuccessful laugh.

"I don't know what to say, Cynthia. I don't know what you'd like me to say." Her eyes were on the slim, bare thighs, on the swelling curves of hips which the skin-tight nylon panties revealed as much as concealed.

"Then say what you think," Cynthia said a bit crossly. *Why* did Jan watch her in that particular way? Both times when she had to undress in front of her, Cynthia had felt a strange, tense aura of sexuality about them. It was almost, at times...yes, almost as though Jan were not of her own sex.

"He appears—competent," Jan said. She flicked her cigaret lighter into flame. "I suppose he's handsome, and I suppose some women would find him charming. Will that do?"

Cynthia ignored the rather waspish tone of Jan's last words. She was coming to accept a certain brusque, almost rude, manner which sometimes seemed to be part of Jan's make-up.

"That's about what I expected you to say," she replied. "Perhaps because that's how I find him."

"Competent, handsome, charming," Jan said, almost to herself.

"To *some* women," Cynthia reminded her. She hurried into the sun-backed dress she was to wear first, and turned to let Jan fasten it.

"You don't like men very much, do you?" Jan asked off-handedly.

Cynthia thought about that.

"I don't like *any* man very much," she said, "with the possible exception of my father. I'm not sure about him."

Bill was ready for them when they reappeared. He had his camera set up before a white-painted, rustic fence with a mailbox on one post, and, after an approving nod, directed Cynthia into position. He rechecked his lights with an exposure meter, explaining small details of his work as he became involved in them. Then, so subtly that she was hardly aware of it, he led her mind away from the unfamiliar equipment, the bulky paraphernalia of the studio, and tried to help her capture the mood of the picture he was visualizing. He spoke of the country, of green fields lying warm under the summer sun, of a girl who was waiting for a letter.

"Close your eyes and try to see yourself there," he said. He turned on a fan, and a light breeze stirred Cynthia's feather-soft hair and gave life and movement to the static folds of the summer dress. "Now listen hard for the mail truck. When I give the word, I want you to look down the road for it, and for no reason at all I want you to say 'whistle.' "

Moments later the click of the shutter marked the successful end of the phantasy.

"I blinked," Cynthia confessed. At that moment she would scarcely have been astonished if a mail truck *had* appeared.

"*After* the shutter clicked. I was watching. You just stay in the country where you belong."

Rapidly changing plates, he began building a word picture of the next situation. He thrust a package and a handful of letters upon her. The mail had arrived, he explained, and for some reason she was now to say "prunes."

In less than five minutes he had taken half a dozen shots in that setting, and "cheese" had been added to Cynthia's somewhat irrelevant bits of dialogue in the playlet. He sent her back to change for the next group.

"Having fun?" Jan asked as she clothes-pinned a tuck in the waist of the new costume.

"It's exciting. But I'm not as self-conscious as I expected to be. He has a way of putting people at ease, don't you think?"

"He knows his work," Jan admitted, in a nearly grudging way.

Cynthia modeled two more outfits after that—a tennis suit and a wonderfully flaring party dress. It lacked a few minutes of being six o'clock when she appeared in the last of the lot, which was a thin cotton print intended for casual wear.

Bill outlined the situation—she was entertaining some friends who had unexpectedly dropped in from a Sunday drive— and she took her place, holding a tea tray. The lights went on, one after another. Then, in the middle of a sentence, Bill Barton stopped talking. Cynthia heard Jan gasp, and a silence so thick it could have been cut in slices fell over the studio. Across the blinding bank of lights, Bill's face looked frozen in startlement. Then some of the lights went out again.

"I'm afraid that won't do," Bill's voice came, a stifled croak.

"What's the matter?" Cynthia asked, ready, as was her habit, to blame herself for whatever it was.

"The back-lighting shines through the dress," Bill explained in a more natural voice. "Peek-a-boo, we saw you."

"I never saw quite so much of anyone so fully clothed," Jan said, twinkling with malice-tinged mischief at Cynthia's instant reddening. "Really, Mr. Barton, she's not *entirely* to be photo-graphed, is she?"

Bill ran distracted fingers through his hair. Jan's laugh was water rippling coolly over pebbles. She was enjoying the situa-tion to the fullest, like a dozing cat who wakes to find a head-in-clouds mouse strolling inches from her nose.

"Mr. Barton," she told Cynthia, "is trying to think up something diplomatic to say. If he'd surprised you in your tub, for instance, he could simply say, 'Excuse me, *sir*,' and back out. But right now there's no place to back into. He provided the setting, the lights, the dress—a put-up job if I ever saw one. That's the sort of thing they've been turning out up in New Haven the last few years."

"Princeton not Yale," he corrected. "Go ahead, have fun. I'll think up a good one in a couple of days. But don't be surprised if the Mafia sends you a few threatening notes in the meantime. I have friends in high places." He darkened the set. "Well, we might as well end on this cheery note. If they didn't send a slip along with the outfit, we might as well forget it for now."

"*I'm* wearing a slip, Mr. Barton," Jan drawled. She put one foot on a chair, turned her skirt back, and displayed the slip, along with a generous expanse of well-shaped leg. "Cynthia can wear it if you want to finish up."

Some wordless exchange seemed to pass between the two. Jan was watchful, half-amusedly expectant. Bill was interested, then wary. His mind seemed to be circling about an unforeseen and not unpleasant possibility, like a cautious fox who discovers a suspiciously obvious delicacy in the leaves along his run.

"I think we'll pass up the offer," he said. "Cynthia has already worked a full day, and I rushed her pretty fast tonight."

"As you like," Jan shrugged, flipping her skirt down.

She was chuckling softly as she helped Cynthia make the final change back to street clothes. Hardly a dozen words were spoken, Cynthia being silent and preoccupied with her own disturbing thoughts, and Jan apparently well enough satisfied with her teasing to be willing to say no more.

While Cynthia was giving her seams a final straightening, Jan remembered that she had left her purse in her office.

"You and Mr. Barton have your own business to attend to," she said, "so I'll trot over and wait for you there. Those releases you're to sign are O.K., incidentally. Just the usual form."

She left Cynthia in Bill's office and went out.

"A weirdy, that one," Bill said. "I wonder where her money comes from?"

"Why, from the business," Cynthia said, surprised that such an obvious matter should be subject to speculation.

"I see." Bill studied some private thought, and then said, "Business must be good. Do you have any idea how much it would cost to buy and equip an operation like that? What bank would back, to any extent, a project as speculative as the thing she's apparently got there? Look at the size of her staff—hell, she has more help than customers. The customers she does have must spend a fortune. And, speaking of fortunes—"

He opened a book of checks and, while Cynthia signed picture releases, made one out. When he had waved it dry, he dropped in on the desk in front of her. Cynthia was somewhat startled by the sum.

"Is this for just one hour?" she asked.

"That's my usual rate for a job like this," he reassured her. "Don't worry, I'm not playing Santa Claus."

"Now I know why girls want to be models." She gathered her things. "Thank you very much, Mr. Bar—Bill. Good night."

"Thank you, Cynthia. And Cynthia—a word of advice, if you don't mind. Just remember what you saw happen with those sets tonight. With a few props you can make a lot of things seem like something they're not."

CHAPTER SEVEN

A WEEK passed. A week in which, for Cynthia, the days were busy and short, the nights long with her loneliness. After that night when Jan had accompanied her to Bill Barton's studio and later, both at dinner and again at her office, briskly discussed business, the two had met and spoken—always briefly—only in the course of their normal working routine. After five each day, Cynthia usually walked about in her own Village neighborhood, losing herself, sometimes in the quaint, twisting streets, and then, after a solitary meal, either dropped into a movie or went home to read and to write lengthy letters to friends. Nowhere, she soon learned, was it possible to be more alone than in the heart of a teeming city—a truism which never seems banal to those who are poignantly living it for the first time. And then Jan had called her at the gym to suggest another dinner date to discuss something new which was coming up.

Now Jan Carter's Cadillac convertible roared across town like an angry bull, scattering pedestrians and private cars with equal success. Buses and taxis fared somewhat better, but even here the more timid gave her a respectable berth.

"Whew!" Cynthia whistled softly as an apparently inevitable crash was avoided by a maneuver which carried them out of danger by mere inches.

"Frightened?" Jan asked. "You needn't be. I drive hard and I drive fast, but I also drive well. It's the ones who aren't quite sure of what they want to do next, the to-be-or-not-to-be boys, who have accidents."

They pulled up before a restaurant on Forty-ninth Street, and Jan locked the car. It was one of those traditional cozy places with checked tablecloths and few customers, and Cynthia noticed that Jan seemed to be known to the people who ran it.

"We want a corner table, Charlie," Jan told the waiter who dog-trotted up to them. "Someplace quiet, where we can do some paperwork." Aside, she mentioned to Cynthia, "The food is good, but not so good that it takes all your attention."

A satisfactory table was found. They ordered, and then plunged into a discussion of Cynthia's work while they waited.

"I can't say that there's any great future in what you're doing now," Jan warned at one point. "The job is as permanent as the business but it doesn't go much of anywhere." She summoned the waiter to order a bottle of Bordeaux, then went on, "You'll make more money as you go along, of course, but if I'm any judge, you'll be heading for bigger things than I can offer you. Or perhaps you just plan to marry and settle down. By the way, and apropos of nothing, have you seen your Mr. Barton lately?"

The waiter brought the wine, uncorked it, and poured a thimbleful for Jan's approval. After she tasted it and nodded, he first filled Cynthia's glass and then finished with Jan's. It was a grave and curious little ceremony which Cynthia had never seen before, and later she watched it repeated at another table where a young married couple was seated, and there, of course, it was the man who approved the wine.

"Where were we?" Cynthia asked as the waiter retreated. "Bill Barton. Yes, I ran into him a couple of times. Once we had lunch and he showed me proofs of the pictures. He's promised me some final prints when they're ready."

She tasted her wine. She knew next to nothing about wines, and found this one rather too tart for her taste. Yet there was a clean, grapey after-tang, and the slight warmness it brought was pleasant. She continued to sip at it now and then, washing down bits of bread with it.

"No more modelling sessions?"

"Not yet. He said something about Saturday afternoon, but it's not definite."

Two heaping dishes of chicken cacciatore arrived then, and over them they discussed a new series of exercises to be started on the following week. Diagrams and procedure sheets gradually covered the table, and in her absorption Cynthia filled her glass again and again, innocently unaware that she was drinking more than she should.

When the last bit of salad had been nibbled, after a demitasse and a cigaret, Jan gathered the papers and called for the check.

"My treat," she said decisively as Cynthia tried to see the bill. "No arguments. I'll charge it off my income tax as a business expense. Big deal."

"You must have some very heavy business expenses," Cynthia suggested, rashly curious. "In fact, I don't see how you keep up with them, now that I know what the courses cost and have some idea of the number of women taking them."

Jan looked at her very sharply. "You're not required to do my bookkeeping," she snapped. More mildly, she added, "But I suppose I don't mind letting you in on the Big Secret. The Fifth Avenue house actually doesn't make any money, even though you'll find things moving pretty fast in the front beauty salon. The mansion is just a showcase, my dear, popular with a handful of rich-witches who don't know what to do with their money. The juicy pickin's lie in the hundreds of thousands of women who aren't in that class or anything like it. And, because they're impressed by the glamour of it all, they buy:—" she counted off on her fingers, "home courses with phonograph records. Home courses with instruction books. Diets to lose weight. Diets to put it back on again. House of Cimier cosmetics—expensive, but what gal won't save up to buy beauty in a bottle?"

They went through the restaurant, Cynthia trailing abashedly. She felt guilty of some stupid gaucherie, although she had

not intended to pry. And, vaguely, she felt annoyed with Bill
Barton for having first brought the question of Jan's finances to
her mind.

But an ugly street scene, meeting them as they left the place,
quickly pushed that line of thought aside. A man and a woman,
both of that type whose thin lips and hard, darting eyes tell of
a dull and sordid succession of precarious years in mouldering
rooming houses and rattletrap hotels, were noisily quarreling.
The woman whined in a shrill excitement; the man gesticulated
and threatened. Then, wildly, the woman leaped forward, claw-
ing at the dark stubble on the man's cheeks. His upthrown elbow
struck her across her mouth, and she dropped to the sidewalk,
dragging at his coat as she fell. Just as he turned, as though in his
rage to strike her even then, Cynthia saw his expression.

For one horrible instant she thought she saw the face of Jake
snarling across at her. Another second, and she knew him to be
a stranger. But the shock contained in that eternity-long watch-
tick of time was more than her senses could stand. The curious
crowd of bystanders faded like phantom figures, and she fainted.

Gradually, as the calm insisting voice spoke her name again and
again, she realized that she was sprawled across the back seat of a
car. Jan's car, and it was Jan talking to her and holding something
to her nostrils that stung her eyes and made her catch her breath.
She waved the something aside and sat up giddily.

"Keep your head low," Jan was saying. "Just bend forward."
And then, "Thank you Charlie," and, "Drink this, Cynthia."

Somehow she choked down the brandy, although it was a
large glass and seemed to have no bottom.

"I never...never did such a...thing...in my...life." She
heard her own voice as through a rainspout. "So stupid. So stupid. So stupid. So—"

"That's enough of that," Jan said severely, a mother with a naughty child, a busy nurse with a recalcitrant patient. "Or shall we try this again?"

She threatened Cynthia with this something again.

"I'll be good," Cynthia promised giggling. "I'll just sit here with my head on the floor and be as good as gold. Why do I have to try to stand on my head. Jan? Am I being punished?"

"You're being silly, and you're babbling. Make yourself comfortable back there. I'm driving you home."

"But I don't *want* to go home. I want to sit in the restaurant some more and talk with Jan. I don't *like* to go home," she scolded. "There's a lamp there that winks at me every time it thinks I'm not looking."

"We're going to my place." Jan said briefly. "Just keep talking to me, but remember, you get five demerits for every two words of nonsense."

"I'll be very solemn. Like in church. Like when they play 'The Star-Spangled Banner'. Like when that fat Mrs. Hinkley tries to jump rope." She giggled again and turned her face to the cushion, feeling the tears start, thin and hot, over her cheeks. "Oh Jan, I feel so damn miserable," she said.

Jan lived on Park Avenue, in the Seventies, but the drive took only a few racing minutes. Pulling up at an impressive apartment house, she helped Cynthia from the car and turned the keys over to the doorman. They crossed a long, handsomely paneled foyer with marble pillars, and entered one of the elevators. Cynthia clutched Jan's arm with a bird-like grip, trying, before the operator, to behave in a perfectly natural way. Actually, as is true in most such cases, she failed, but her failure was of no importance. The elevator man, though he might roll his eyes speculatively, was a thoughtful man who kept his own counsel and two cats, and his mind was on his collection of match-book covers, which was one of the finest in the East.

Jan's apartment was a large duplex on the sixteenth floor, the set-back forming her terrace. Even in her present distraught condition, Cynthia was impressed by it. Her own background had hardly been one of poverty, and she was accustomed to living in an atmosphere of good things; the flawless taste of the apartment's furnishing was not lost on her, nor was the fact that such an impeccable blending of the finest in antique and modern craftsmanship could not have been achieved at less than fantastic cost. The first rug her foot touched she recognized as a real Kirman-Lavehr, and it set the keynote of the symphony for living which Jan had made of the place. And yet Jan Carter had protested that she was not wealthy!

Jan touched a button, and a scatter of lamps glowed softly. Leading Cynthia to a couch, she took her things as though she were dealing with a child.

"Just sit there quietly, now," she said. "I'll get you some cognac." She opened an ancient Chinese cabinet and revealed its conversion to a tiny liquor bar.

"I've had more than I'm used to already," Cynthia protested listlessly. "That's probably why I did that silly thing."

"Unh-unh," Jan shook her head. "Don't try to tell me that you passed out. Something big is bothering you, and I've sensed it for some time. If ever a girl was in a state where she ought to get a bit tight, you're in it. If you don't want to drink it, just hold the glass; you'll find it a big comfort."

She browsed briefly among a tremendous collection of phonograph records, selected an album, and set the player in operation.

"I think you'll find Debussy very therapeutic," she smiled, setting the controls so that the music, while it could be plainly heard was definitely in the background. "Now." She sat down in a nearby easy chair and turned her own glass slowly in her hand. "Let's talk about you. Just talking about things sometimes does a lot to clear them up. Heaven knows I don't want to play psychiatrist, but it could be that I can help in other ways."

"It's just—oh, it's one of those things that get stuck so deeply inside you that you don't even try to talk about it. You just wish that part of your life had never been lived, and you try to pretend that it wasn't."

"A man, Cynthia?" Jan asked quietly.

A man! was Cynthia's immediate thought. Not a man, a beast, foul and reeking of his own filth! But she only nodded and touched her lips to the pungent sting of the cognac.

"You're not pregnant," Jan mused, not asking a question, but stating a fact known to her.

"Oh God!" Cynthia exclaimed, her voice breaking on the edge of an hysterical laugh. For some reason she had never considered that her experience with Jake might very easily have resulted in the quickening of an alien and unloveable life within her. "Oh God, if *that* had happened … "

"So already we see that things might have been worse," Jan said persuasively. "There are probably all kinds of unconsidered possibilities with which you aren't burdened. But let's not be Pollyannas. Cynthia, it is difficult to tell anyone, directly, that you want to be her friend. Friendship just grows, like Topsy. But there are times, there are situations, in which one woman needs another desperately. Sometimes it is hard to know who profits more in the giving of a confidence, for our lives are made up of strange needs and unfathomable hungers. So let me say it: I hope, Cynthia, that you can accept me as your friend, for I may need the reassurance of your confidence more than you can realize."

The quiet swirl of remembered things which had never been whisperingly throated across the room as the music recalled a legend and a dream. Alcohol spun a web of unreality across Cynthia's world.

"I've never told anyone," she said, so softly that she spoke almost to herself. "Not anyone, ever."

She raised her glass and swallowed burning, grapey courage. Jan, watchful, jabbed a cigarette against a table top and snapped her lighter open.

"There was a stable," said Cynthia. "The shadow of a man ... "

Long before she had finished the telling of that story, Jan had snubbed out the smoke and was at her side. Jan's arms went strongly about her, reassuring firmness in which her spasmodic shudders spent themselves. Jan's shoulder offered warmth and secrecy for her face, Jan's throat and breast received her tears. She felt Jan's fingertips' light stroke on her temples, the brush of Jan's lips against her hair. And, whispering, comforting, she heard Jan's voice, "Cynthia ... Cynthia ... "

Cynthia blew her nose on a large handkerchief which Jan gave her. She tried to sit up straight, but found that it was a problem. The room was not spinning, but the wall was moving rapidly to the right and the moulding of the ceiling was moving slowly to the left.

"You poor thing," Jan was saying in a voice torn with sympathy. "I had no idea ... and to think I teased you about what happened at Barton's ... oh, Cynthia, I'm dreadfully sorry!"

Cynthia stood up, weaving erratically. "I'm tight, Jan," she informed her unnecessarily. "Cynthia's tight as a tick."

"You're going to stay right here tonight," Jan said, "so it doesn't matter a bit. Into the bedroom with you now."

Cynthia protested, but it was more an automatic matter of form than a real desire to do otherwise. Tonight, of all nights, she did not want to return to her room downtown. She allowed herself to be led to a bedroom, here she sat down heavily on an oversized Hollywood bed. Fingers pressed to her temples, she rocked unsteadily until Jan, with a puckish expression, tipped her backward with a light push from a single finger.

She heard her shoes drop to the floor. Then she felt her skirt being pushed upward, felt Jan unfastening her garters. She closed her eyes so that she would not have to watch the motion of the ceiling. Everything that happened seemed to be very far away, and it happened in jerks, like the action in a movie that has been cut.

She was sitting up again, and for an instant she smothered as her slip was drawn up over her head. Then her brassiere was gone and she was lying down once more. Time ticked away in silence. It seemed like ages. She felt a stir of uneasiness.

"Jan?" She spoke without opening her eyes.

"Yes, Cynthia."

"I wondered if you were still here."

Jan's fingers were at her sides, tugging the tight panties downward. She raised her hips to help. And then she was naked. Again that silence. She turned restlessly on her side. Jan's hand touched her hair strokingly, then moved down to the nape of the neck. With a touch that was almost a caress, Jan massaged the little lines of muscle down to her shoulders.

"Jan, I have something else to tell you," Cynthia said abruptly, and very seriously.

"Yes … "

"I haven't been getting my rub-downs," she confessed solemnly. "Or is it rubs-down?"

Jan laughed. "You seem to be bearing up well."

"I don't like Mary what's-her-name much. And as for Arthur—he actually *punishes* some of those women, Jan. And they go back to him every day."

"Arthur fulfills his duties very thoroughly," Jan said as though in agreement, "probably because he enjoys his work. Yes, he caters to a very demanding clientele."

She turned back the coverlet and prepared the bed.

"Do you want pajamas?" she asked doubtfully. "I have some about somewhere, but I usually sleep raw."

"I'm fine this way," Cynthia replied in a voice which was thickening with drowsiness. She slid between the cool sheets and reached out one hand to take Jan's. Jan sat down beside her.

"You're being awfully kind, Jan. And I do feel better, now that I've told you about . . . that."

For reply Jan lifted her hand to her lips and kissed it. Then she bent over and kissed her cheek.

Suddenly it was all so warm and wonderful and affectionate that Cynthia wanted to cry again this time from relief and gratitude. But she did not. Instead she drifted quietly to sleep, while Jan stroked her hair and murmured softly.

CHAPTER EIGHT

COULD she somehow have known the pattern of Jan's movements after she fell asleep, Cynthia would have been a very puzzled girl indeed. For some time after she was certain the Cynthia slept, Jan continued to sit by her side. Her eyes, no longer veiled by the mask of reassuring calm which she had turned to Cynthia, were bright with a kind of anxiety. Her fingers, when she raised them to toss back a lock of her short-cut hair, could have been seen to tremble ever so slightly. She studied the girl's now placid face with a lover's jealous seeking. Finally she arose, turned the table lamp to its lowest intensity, and left the bedroom.

In the living room she turned the radio on, hung a cigaret on her lip, and restlessly padded the floor in that curious, lengthy stride. She walked out on the terrace and looked out at the lights of the city, tossed the cigaret away when it scorched her fingers, and watched it spiral down, trailing sparks to the street.

"Damn it!" she said aloud, as though in argument, "She's such a kid!"

She went back to the living room and poured herself a drink, which she set down and forgot.

(Where did it start? And does that matter now? Come on, Jan, you're a smart girl. You've read the books; you know the answers. You know the answers upside down and backward, as well as inside out. You can almost spot the very minute when you dropped out of competition with your mother. You know what makes you this way. But what to do about it—they left that page out of the book. And there wasn't any chapter on the ethics of your position. Nothing about what to do when a hurt and frightened kid comes into your life, and you don't want to see her hurt in any way, any more. You love her, you say, but the books say you don't love her. You can have her, this innocent; you can start her down that endless road of brief affection and suddenly rejection which you know so well. And someday, after a succession of flaring promises and disappointments, she will be, you know, almost exactly where you are. Because you're not quite phoney enough to pretend to yourself that this will be permanent, any more than the others were. But why should you let that bother you? Why is permanency of so much importance? None of them matter now. Count them off on your fingers, from that first school-girl crush on the history teacher who was no Lesbian, really, but just curious. Not one of them matters now. So could it be because ... because ... ?)

"I'm so damned lonely!" Jan said to the radio. And now she remembered her drink, and she took it up and set the glass down empty. Then she put on her coat and scribbled a short note which she left on the night table beside Cynthia, and quietly left the apartment.

She took a cab downtown to the Village, left the cab at a Sixth Avenue corner, and walked the two blocks from there. As she strode along a man fell in step with her and spoke. Without looking at him, she muttered sharply out of her mouth. He stopped, then, and let her walk on.

"Hell," he said to the night, "every time I go out shopping for fish, they got a special on meat. I shoulda stood in Brooklyn."

At a bar lighted by a sign which bore a woman's name, she turned in. The place was crowded with women, some in slacks, some in mannishly cut suits, and a great many in completely feminine dress. There were almost no men. Jan pushed her way to the bar and ordered a drink. While she waited, she kept her eyes on the bar mirror, making a measured study of the girl who was sitting on the bar stool beside her. Then her drink arrived, and as she was paying for it, she could feel the girl turn and look at her face from the side. She looked up.

"Hello," she said. "May I buy you a drink?"

The girl was rather large, with a soft body which gave an impression of white and pink. Her hair was blonde and shoulder length, and her brows were plucked so that she looked at the world in continual, delicate surprise. Around one fine-boned ankle, she wore a fragile gold chain, and her shoes were open-toed platforms with exaggerated heels.

"Thank you, but I'm with a friend," she said in a husky voice in which a throbbing sensuality seemed to undulate. "She'll be back in a minute."

"Aren't you allowed to be with another friend in the meantime?"

"She doesn't like me to be with other people when we're out together. It makes her sad, and when she is sad she is very nasty."

Jan noticed a dark, small bruise on the white forearm.

"I do not much like people who get nasty," Jan said. "It doesn't seem like a good way to enjoy yourself."

"That's what I like," the girl said. "I like to have a good time. I like to have a good time and enjoy myself, and not get sad and nasty like that, but a lot of things make her sad."

"Is she being sad now?" asked Jan.

"I think she is being sick. That makes her sad too."

"She sounds like one sad sack," Jan said. "Let's get out of this place and go to another place where we can have a good time with the drinking, enjoying ourselves and talking like Hemingway some more. How do you feel? Do you feel fine? You have to feel very fine to talk like Mr. Hemingway."

"I feel pretty good."

"Pretty good isn't bad. Pretty good is all right."

"I think I could feel better if I started to have a good time."

"That's fine. You just keep that up and you'll be all right."

"What are we talking about, anyway?" the girl wanted to know. "Are you making fun of me?"

Jan took her arm and she slid from the stool.

"I couldn't make fun of you if I tried. You're unbelievable. Shall we go?"

"We'd better hurry before she comes back."

Outside, they started down the street. Jan was watching for a cab, but none came into sight. They had gone about a half block when running footsteps sounded behind them. A woman in slacks and a suede jacket caught the girl's dodging shoulder and began shaking her.

"You little slut!" she cried. "Every time my back's turned you pull something like this! But you don't get away with it this time! Not this time, you—"

Jan waited until the blow was descending. Almost lazily, then, she picked the woman's wrist out of the air and used the force of the blow to spin the woman toward her and into a waist-held, jabbing fist. The woman doubled over and backed against the wall for support.

"Keep—keep out of this, butch," the woman gasped. "I can take you too, if I have to."

A prowl car pulled up soundlessly. Lieutenant James O'Rourke and Sergeant Edward Manetti considered the scene with professional interest. Sergeant Manetti tugged the remains of a candy bar from his teeth.

"Coupla dikes," he commented. "Just another dike brawl. Goddamit."

He got out of the car and went over to them.

"I'm gettin' damn fed up with this stuff," he said. "This time we're all going to take a little ride and talk with the man at the desk."

"Just a moment, officer," Jan said. She opened her purse and took out a card. Sergeant Manetti looked at it and then handed it back. Then he looked at Jan.

"Friend of *his,* huh? Guess it takes all kinds. Well, you wanta prefer charges?"

"Does *she* want to prefer charges?" the woman yelled. "Does *she* want to prefer charges?"

"Shuddup. I seen the whole thing. If you don't keep your trap closed, maybe I'll prefer charges myself, much as I hate to get up for ten o'clock court."

"All I want is a taxi," Jan said. She saw the lights of one as it turned the corner and came toward them. "I'll bet you five dollars you can't find me one."

Sergeant Manetti waved down the cab. "You lose."

"Thank you," Jan said, extending her hand.

Sergeant Manetti shook hands enthusiastically and closed his fist over the bill. Jan and the girl entered the cab.

"What's your address?" she asked the girl.

"Let's go to that other bar first and *then* go home," the girl said. She was very soft and very feminine, but she knew when to be firm also.

At that exact instant, the phone was ringing in Jan's apartment. Cynthia struggled out of sleep, groggily fumbling for the extension on the table and at the same time reading the curt note waiting for her:

Out on a lengthy errand. Don't wait up. If you can't sleep, take two pills with water.

Cynthia brushed the pills aside.

"Hello."

"Jan?" The voice knowing that it was not.

"Jan's out on an errand. Is there a message?"

"Who is this?"

"Cynthia Bennett. Is there a—"

The phone went dead. That had been Meg. Or had it? Cynthia could not be sure. She rolled over and went back to sleep.

It seemed like hours later when a careful movement in the room awakened her for the second time. Not stirring, she opened one eye and saw Jan undressing and trying to be quiet about it. She watched Jan's naked movements about the room with sleepy interest, watched the almost boyishly trim body move away toward the bathroom. For a long time she heard the shower running before Jan came back, scrubbed and glowing.

"Jan..."

"I thought I was being quiet."

"There was a call while you were out. No message." She wriggled across the bed. "Am I taking up all the room?"

Jan picked up a brush and began pushing it roughly through her hair.

"Wouldn't you sleep better alone?" Jan asked. "I can just as well use the other bedroom."

"No. I think I'd feel better if you were right here."

She had been thinking about that while Jan was in the shower. Wondering if she could stand having another person in her bed, another body against hers. And it seemed almost disloyal to wonder about that when the other person was Jan, who was being so kind, who was so understanding and gentle with her. No, whatever had been strained and unnatural between Jan and herself had been of her own making. She had found a wonderful warm and helpful friend, and she was determined not to let their relationship be threatened by some darkening miasma from the past. So she stretched out now and closed her eyes as though the question had been discussed and settled and was too slight to think about any further.

She felt the covers being drawn back, and the bed settled a bit as it received Jan's body. Light flicked into darkness, and in the silence she could hear Jan's breathing. She stirred, and her thighs touched against Jan's rigid flank. Jan stirred too. Had she drawn away? No, the touch of her skin was back again, warmness and smoothness, with the flesh tensed beneath.

"Jan?"

"Cynthia?"

"Good night, Jan—and thank you."

"Good night, you silly."

Turning, now Cynthia put her hand doubtfully on Jan's shoulder and pushed her nose close to her hair. A breath of musky sweetness there was unexpected—she had been sure that Jan did not use perfumes, or at least not that heavy, sultry type.

"Do you mind?" she asked.

"No, Cynthia, I don't mind."

Contentedly and happy, Cynthia went back to sleep.

CHAPTER NINE

"HOW do you feel?" Jan, already dressed, was touching her face with what little make-up she wore.

"As though I were wearing the wrong size head," Cynthia replied. She sat up in bed and turned her head carefully from side to side. "It doesn't work as well as the old one," she announced.

"That can be fixed," Jan said. She went into the bathroom and came out soon with a glass of something that was green and fizzy.

"You seem to have a remedy for everything," Cynthia said. "Will I live, Doctor?"

"Breakfast and some air will complete the cure," Jan promised. "My woman came in a few minutes ago, and I think I smell coffee now."

As usual, Jan was right. By the time they were dropping to street level in the elevator, Cynthia was humming lightheartedly, and the cool morning air soon restored the normal color to her cheeks as the brute Caddy, top down, zoomed them toward the big brownstone.

Jan stopped as they came to the corner.

"No need for both of us to walk from the parking lot," she said. "And I've got a stop or two to make on the way back."

Cynthia hopped out and blithely trotted to the door. Meg was just going in, apparently having come up the street unobserved as they arrived. Cynthia caroled a greeting.

"Oh, hello," Meg said in a tone so dead and hostile that the effect like running into a brick wall.

Nothing more was said, for the intention was obviously to block any further communication, civil or otherwise. Cynthia went directly to her own work, and gradually lost herself in its many small problems. Toward the end of the morning she received an outside phone call from Bill, suggesting a luncheon date. She accepted, and would have been glad to prolong the call—because, she told herself, a friendly phone call was such a rare thing for her, now that she had eight and a half million neighbors—but an emergency interrupted. The mechanical horse had gone berserk, and Miss Pottle, trimming down for her forthcoming marriage, was in imminent danger of losing a great deal more than just the fifteen pounds she had bargained for.

At noon she and Bill walked to the cafeteria on Lexington Avenue. When they were seated he handed over a brown envelope which he had been carrying.

"Those prints I promised you," he said. "And, by the way, this catalogue job is being held up for several days, so we can call off that session for this Saturday. See now why so many models look underfed?"

"You can't scare me," Cynthia said. "I have a *real* job, the kind where you eat every day. Now I can use Saturday to hunt for an apartment."

Up to the moment when she spoke, Cynthia had not known that it was her intention to move. But, once the thought had been expressed, she knew that she was unable to live any longer in the drab room which she had hastily rented an hour or so after stepping off the train which had carried her to the city. Between the dark hole into which she had been crawling every night, and the expensive freedom of Jan's place, the contrast was so great and the effect upon her spirit so marked that she was forced to realize into what an unnecessarily stifling and depressing atmosphere she had unthinkingly thrust herself.

She tried to explain it to Bill.

"I wanted to be entirely on my own, do you see? My family would help me out to any extent I might ask—but I wanted to feel that I was living on myself, living just the way I'd have to live if they weren't there. I have to know that I'm not dependent on them any more. Am I making sense? Do you understand?"

"If I didn't," Bill answered, "I wouldn't be doing what I'm doing now—I'd be helping my father run some of his paper mills. After all, when I was sent to college, no one expected that six months after graduation I'd be knocking on doors trying to sell photography."

"Well, now that I'm working for Jan, I can afford something better than this room I'm in now. And I think I *need* another place to live, someplace with another room to go into, and maybe a door to slam if I feel like it. I felt so free in her place. For the first time since I've been in New York, I didn't feel cramped."

"Oh—you've actually been to her apartment, then?"

"Yes, I ... spent last night there." And, flustered lest the reason for her being there somehow enter the discussion, Cynthia went into a lengthy description of the place.

"Sounds rather opulent," Bill finally observed. "And I still can't see how she meets her payroll."

"I don't like that in you," Cynthia said. "That's the second time you've said something which sounded almost as though you suspected her of—I don't know. Robbing widows and orphans, maybe."

And, earnestly, she went on to explain the various sources of income which Jan had outlined to her.

"All right, all right, all right!" Bill exclaimed, raising his hands in mock surrender. "I give up. I will write five hundred times: 'I will never again idly speculate on the source of my neighbor's income'. I just wish I had the knack of turning a buck that easily. Jealous, that's me."

But, as they walked back to Fifth Avenue, an odd thing happened.

"Cigarets," Bill said. "I'm almost out."

They entered a large drugstore of the type which has never run a one-cent sale, nor failed to display two apothecaries' jars of colored water in its window. And here, while Bill was busy at the cigaret counter, Cynthia found a display of House of Cimier cosmetics. She browsed through them, dawdling until Bill rejoined her.

"Look. Fancy house I work for." She pointed out an ounce bottle of perfume priced at twenty dollars.

Noting their interest, a man came up behind the counter, looking more patient than expectant. He evidently knew Bill, and nodded in recognition.

"At these prices, we're looking, not buying," Bill said. "Mere professional curiosity. This is a pretty good line, isn't it?"

A shrug. "You told the whole story, Bill. A good line that people look at and don't buy."

"I thought House of Cimier was pretty popular," Bill argued.

"It pays for the space it takes up. You notice we don't give it much space. Trouble is—well, take this perfume. It doesn't have the name Chanel Number Five has, or even Twenty-Two. But it's priced right up there. Priced right past its reputation and its own market. Same thing with everything they put out-priced right up with the leaders; reputation nowhere near the top."

"But the dealer gets a good break, is that it?"

"The best. We make more on one of these items than anything in the case, and that's the only reason we touch the line at all. At the price they make us, it doesn't hurt so much if it moves slow. See, the salesman explained it to me once—they just use this for advertising, to keep their name in front of the public. They've got a big place over on Fifth, and the real money comes out of that."

"I get it. They just want to break even."

"That's it, just advertising. Say, listen," he leaned conspiratorially toward Bill, "if you're interested, I can give you a break on some of this stuff. Say, five dollars for that bottle of perfume."

Bill whistled. "You can go that low, can you?"

"Five dollars. Sold?"

"This young lady," Bill said severely, "is an employee of The House of Cimier. She is a spotter, and is weeding out the chiselers. You are prepared for a law-suit and possible prosecution, I suppose?"

The other jumped back as though on strings.

"I never said it!" he protested. "You must have misunderstood me. I—aw, you're giving me the needle," he finished sheepishly.

Bill took Cynthia's arm and led her gaily to the door. There he stopped and, pointing an accusing finger at his victim, called in a stentorian voice,

"Bigamy is a serious charge, sir! Mark my words, you will be ordered by the courts to contribute in some way to the support of the three little tykes!"

Leaving the druggist laughing hollowly in an effort to convince the startled customers that it was all a joke, Bill steered Cynthia out of the place. They had gone almost a block before she spoke.

"You're feeling awfully smart, aren't you?"

"Not particularly. I didn't notice any great brain-work being done. I asked a couple of questions and he felt like talking."

"Well, I don't like it. For some reason that I don't understand, you don't like Jan Carter, and you seem determined to create some sort of a situation to discredit her. I am not particularly interested in whatever arrangements Jan's salesmen make with drug clerks. I am interested in her as a person. And I have found her to be generous and good and understanding. But I do not think she could understand you. I do not think she could understand that meanness of spirit which obliges you to keep picking away at some vague insinuation which you yourself can't explain. Or can you? Do you know one single, tangible fact about Jan which would justify the nasty, suspicious way you've been acting about her?"

Bill's words were thoughtfully slow and measured.

"No," he said, "I cannot say that I know one thing about Jan Carter which is to her discredit. I imagine that very few people know anything at all about her."

"Don't bother to build her up as a sloe-eyed woman of mystery. Just tell me why you don't like her."

"You stayed with her last night, didn't you? And you still can't imagine why a man wouldn't like her?"

"I haven't the slightest idea of what you are talking about. More of those hinted mysteries of yours?"

"Let's say that she's in my way."

"In *your* way? For heaven's sake, how?"

"Oh hell," he exclaimed. "Can't we just drop it? You don't know what I'm talking about, and I'm not even sure that I do. Let's not quarrel about Jan Carter."

The rest of their time together was made up of that silence which is the more profound for being broken by polite observations on the contents of shop windows and matters of like import.

When she left Bill, Cynthia did not immediately go to the gymnasium. She wanted first to speak to Jan about having Miss Pottle's hobby-horse repaired, as well as to suggest that Miss Pottle herself should be given a gratis half-hour repair job at the hands of Dr. Ramsey, the woman psychologist who came in three days a week to discuss such problems as neurotic obesity. That Miss Pottle had been using such phrases as "traumatic experience", and seemed to hint that if her marriage failed, the House of Cimier would be held directly responsible.

There was no answer when she rapped on the door of Jan's office, but she looked in anyway. Through a second door, which had been left open, she saw the figures of Jan, Dr. Ramsey, and a well-dressed rather frightened-looking woman standing at the end of the hall near the self-service elevator. She hurried toward them, but before she got their attention, all three had gotten into the elevator. Frustrated, she watched the indicator dial swing jerkily up to the figure "3". After a minute she pressed a buzzer and it began its slow descent. By the time she took it up to the third floor again, there was no one in sight.

She had not been on this floor before, and was rather curious to see the lecture rooms Jan had mentioned. She found two, small and looking very much like school class rooms that had seen little use, but both of them were empty. Past these rooms the hallway was blocked by a solid-looking door which showed evidence of having been put in not too long ago. Cynthia tried it. It was locked, and the lock was a Yale.

It seemed like a very illogical place to put such a door.

She half raised her hand to knock, but paused with an uncertainty which she could not have explained. There was something more than illogical about that door. It was forbidding. And it became the more so as the thought came to her that whatever was beyond it—and it represented a considerable amount of space—could not be reached through any other entrance.

She turned away, but not before she had heard a quiet movement, as though someone had come to the other side of the door, had listened, and had then gone away. She walked back to the elevator and took it down to the ground floor.

Another puzzle to ponder over. And one which she knew she would not discuss with Bill.

CHAPTER TEN

FOR Cynthia the next few days fairly flew, as she threw herself into the formidable task of finding and furnishing a suitable apartment. Her spare hours after work were a busy round of studying the newspapers, making phone calls, and dashing on tours of inspection. At last she found what she was looking for—two large rooms with a tiny kitchen and a bath—and set about refurbishing and outfitting them.

She did all the work herself, scrubbing and scouring, mixing paint and patching the plaster, putting up shelving and fastening a loose board here and there. And, piece by piece, even as she was doing the work, she picked up the furnishings.

During this while she had no life outside her job and the work on the apartment. She had told Jan what she was doing, and Jan, approving, had offered to help.

"No," Cynthia shook her head. "I'll surprise you with it when it's done. I want to try to do this alone."

She had no time for lunches with Bill now. She carried a sandwich or two to work, and snatched them when she could, using her lunch hour to gulp a cup of coffee and then scour the shops for the things she needed. Occasionally she caught a glimpse of him as she passed the studio, and once he had spoken to her for a few minutes on the street to ask her how her personal housing project was coming along, but that was all.

Then one day as she rushed home from uptown, Cynthia found that the apartment was finished. For the preceding few evenings she had been engaged in taking care of odds and ends which had been overlooked or put off—fixing a cupboard door, or setting up a new towel rack in the bathroom. Now on this late afternoon as she greeted the kitten she had acquired along with the lease, she found that there was nothing more to do.

She moved a piece of furniture here and there, but it was made work. So she sat down and began going over her budget.

For some time she had known that she was spending more than she had anticipated. However, she had refused to be trapped by the false economy of buying shoddy goods, so she had twice sharply raised her original estimate of the final cost. Checking over bank stubs and receipts, she saw that even her final limit had been passed.

The money she had spent was part of a gift from her father—a sum which she had banked with the intention of using half of it as a revolving fund for such expenditures as the present ones, and reserving the other half for only the gravest emergencies. The halfway mark had been passed by a substantial amount. In her own mind, Cynthia was in the red, and it annoyed her. She had planned that, by returning a large part of her salary to the account, she would replace the entire sum within a set number of weeks, and now she would be unable to keep that promise to herself as banker.

She threw down her pen in disgust.

"I might as well let you take care of my money," she told the kitten who now purred on her lap. "I don't seem to be able to do it for myself."

They sparred, forefinger and paw. "Why don't you go out and get a job?" she nagged. "Hanging around the house all day..."

What about a part-time job for herself? she thought. If she had something to do in the evenings, a few hours a week—

She took up the newspaper and began running through the help-wanted column. And almost at once she found something which interested her:

"Model for evening photography class. Young, pretty, experience not necessary."

She considered the ad. "Experience not necessary" probably meant that they weren't particularly interested in the fakey clothes-horses that Bill had described. And *some* experience, such as the little she had, was bound to be an asset. She decided to call.

She learned very little over the phone. The man who answered was full of questions about her—where did she live, how long had she been in New York, how old was she—but had little information to give. The pay—well, that varied, but the pay was good. Yes, they could give a suitable girl several hours' work a week. The whole thing could be much better explained in a personal interview. That evening, if possible. At eight o'clock. He gave her the address and the name of the place, which had the words "Art" and "School" in it, and rang off.

Eight o'clock found Cynthia climbing the sagging stairs of a neglected loft building on a poorly lighted street in the Twenties. She had by now learned enough about the city's dearth of space to reserve judgment until she had actually seen the "school", but she could not help feeling depressed by the atmosphere of dank mustiness and disregarded litter which formed her first impression of the place.

The office which she entered did little to inspire more confidence. An effort had been made to create out of painted beaver-board and chrome a garish imitation of that decor known as "moderne", with the result that the effect was a doggerel parody of something which had been unworthy to begin with. The man who came out to meet her chewed a dead cigar when he was not chewing his lip.

Cynthia introduced herself, and he nodded and spat a bit of tobacco out of the corner of his mouth. He rolled the cigar from side to side, and seemed to be looking rather than listening. Finally he chomped it to a jaunty, up-tilted position and said.

"Bewitchanaminute. Godagirlageridda."

He went into a smaller office marked "private" in shaky letters, and a minute later ushered out a drab, mousey girl who appeared to be a year or so younger than Cynthia. She was being assured that if an opening turned up, she would be notified. She obviously didn't believe it, nor did the man.

Cynthia went into the smaller office, and as he waved her to a chair, the man struck a match and held it to his cigar. Several times during the interview Cynthia watched him do that, but he never managed to get it lighted.

"This here school," the man said—and then he used the name, including the word "Art". "This here school is recanized for teachin' the est'etics of photography, for which purpose it was endowed. In other words, we concentrate heavy on est'etics, which is to say, like in a art class for painters, only here," he took the cigar from his mouth to let the phrase roll out, "we paint with light." After a proper pause he went on, "The basis of all est'etics is the human form, so naturly we use the human form as the basis of teachin' our students … ah … the basis of est'etics. In other words, the human form is the basis on which we teach our students the est'etic part of the art game, like where to put the lights and like that, and how to bring out the emphasis of concentration on the subject by means of light and shadow." He leaned back and reflected, "But I guess this is all pretty technical talk for you."

Cynthia could have told him that the removal of the cigar might have aided in her understanding of what he was trying to say, but she merely smiled uncertainly and strained to hear what he was saying next. Something about "life classes." Something about "the nude female form."

She stood up.

"I misunderstood," she said. "I didn't know that was what you were looking for."

"But wait a minute!" the man exclaimed, relinquishing the cigar to emphasize his sincerity. "That comes *later*, for the advanced classes. Tonight we got a class that's workin' on how to bring out the emphasis of concentration on different fabrics. See, we have like different dresses, and they learn how to place the lights to—to bring out the emphasis. Oh, I wouldn't want you to think I was asking *you* to ... " He let the rest of the sentence hang, but added, as though to himself, "Of course it *does* pay better."

Cynthia would still have left, but he was ushering her to another room.

"I just want you to look at the costumes," he urged. "Look them over and then make up your mind."

She was taken into a rather large dressing room, the most noticeable features of which were the numerous mirrors of all sizes which were set into three of the walls. Along the fourth wall were wooden chests covered in leatherette, and from these the man began pulling an unmatched assortment of clothing which looked as though it might have come from a theatrical costume house. There was a cow-girl outfit with fringed gauntlets and high boots and two dime-store six-shooters. A can-can outfit with shoulder-length black gloves, long tights, and slippers whose heels would have made it almost impossible to walk. A hoop skirt in the style of the antebellum South, with ankle-length pantaloons. And, as though in afterthought, one brief, but conservative, bathing suit.

"Ah ... I'd like you to wear the bathing suit first," the man said, as though it were settled that Cynthia had now been persuaded to stay. "It's that new dye they're using. It ... ah ... the lights act different on it than regular dyes, and I want the class to see how it photographs." He laid the costumes out on a long, box-like bench which was in almost the exact center of the room and which was also covered in imitation leather. "You can lock the door from the inside," he added in a tone intended to inspire confidence. "And take your time about changing. See, I give a lecture, like, in between the times you're in the studio explaining them what they did wrong. The class starts in ten minutes."

"But—" Cynthia began.

The man, however, was gone. She sat down on the boxlike piece of furniture and thought about it a minute. Then, with a shrug of her shoulders, she went to the door and bolted it and began to undress.

The light in that room was extremely bright. There were, in fact, so many fixtures on the ceiling that she supposed the room had originally been used as a studio, and perhaps still was. And it seemed that everywhere she looked she found herself staring back from one of the mirrors.

She laid her dress out carefully, and then her slip. The bathing suit was backless, so she took her brassiere off also. As for her panties—well, they were of the type which double as a garter belt, and she could certainly not appear in a bathing suit with garters hanging along her thighs.

Naked, she leaned back and stretched, watching her action duplicated by half a dozen reflected images. It was fascinating to see oneself from so many different angles, she thought. It was almost like meeting a stranger who looked somewhat like you, the way it was in the fitting room of a dressmaker's. She pirouetted and studied her full profile, and was reminded suddenly that she once *did* have a nickname, although she had denied it to Bill. At summer camp, for one season, the girls had called her "Bubs".

After she had put on the bathing suit she looked at herself again. It was anything but immodest, she decided, and the rest of the costumes were positively concealing. She might as well go ahead with it, this one time, although she had no intention of coming back again. She slid her feet into the bath sandals which had been provided, put on a flowered kimono, and went out into the studio.

At first she found no one, but the man with the cigar soon appeared, smiling his tobacco-stained approval.

"Now the class will be right in," he said. "You just sit up here on this and make yourself comf'table." He pointed to the model stand and began fussing with lights.

The class consisted of about a dozen men of all ages and appearance. Some of the younger ones were grinning, and there was a great deal of whispering and half-suppressed laughter. All of them held cameras of one type or another, ranging from the cheapest Kodaks to rugged, professional machines.

"Now," the man said, "I guess we're all ready. You all remember what I was tellin' you about this, ah, dye they use, and how tricky it is to bring out the right emphasis on it. So remember to use your lights and shadows and, ah, get the effect. O. K. Let's get to work."

With cameras aimed at her from all possible angles, and some which seemed impossible. Cynthia smiled as directed, and heard a few shutters snap. Then, abruptly, it was all over.

"That's it, fellows" the man said. "Now let's get back to the lecture room while the model prepares."

"That was pretty fast," Cynthia said as she slid from the dais. "I expected several poses for each costume."

"Nope, nope. It's like I told you. Just the emphasis of the fabrics. Now don't hurry about changing. Like I said, I give a little talk in between each pose."

Cynthia went back to the dressing room and removed the bathing suit. Since the cowgirl outfit called for bare legs, she did not put her panties on again, but started to get into the fringed skirt, which was a combination with panties underneath. But something was wrong with the skirt. It had evidently needed some repair, and whoever had done the work had carelessly stitched it so that it was impossible to get into. She took a nail-file from her purse and spent several minutes in pulling out enough stitches so that she could wear it.

Once more she went back to the studio, and the same hurried procedure was repeated. The whispering and laughter was repeated too, but this time more openly. Cynthia decided that she did not like the students any more than the instructor. There was definitely something unpleasant about the whole place, and she had a feeling that something unknown to her was taking place. Something of which she was the center.

After the second brief stay on the modeling stand, Cynthia began to change to the hoop-skirted costume. She wriggled into the pantaloons, which were somewhat tight, and it was not until she had them on that she realized that they were actually only two leggins, somewhat like tights, with nothing to cover the lower part of her torso. She looked at herself in the mirrors. Never had she worn anything which looked more obscene. And, even though the skirts would cover it...

She began to feel panicky. Something was wrong about the "Art" school—very wrong. She did not know what it was, but it was there just the same. Hurriedly, she got into the rest of the costume and went out to look for the man with the cigar.

"I—I just remembered," she said (*How* did he know each time when she came into the studio, when the door through which he and the students entered was solid wood and without glass?), "I just remembered I promised a friend I'd call. May I use the office phone?"

He was reluctant but could hardly refuse. She went into the office and rang Jan's home number. The phone buzzed urgently for several minutes, but there was no answer.

Her panic was growing. She was positive by now that she was in the midst of something unknown and unpleasant, and her confidence in herself was fast ebbing away. She knew only one other person well enough to call. She looked through the book and found his office number and his home number. She called the second.

"Bill? This is Cynthia."

His voice was surprised and glad and reassuring.

"Bill, I'm in some sort of a mess, and I don't know exactly what it is."

"Where are you?" he interrupted immediately. "All right, go on."

She told him about the man with the cigar, the strange students, the costumes and the dressing room.

"Sounds fishy," he agreed. "I'll drive right over. In the meantime, just keep on as you have been, but stall a little. I don't think things will get any rougher than they are right now—not if I'm right about what I think is happening."

He hung up. Cynthia, remembering his advice to stall, stayed at the phone until the man with the cigar came impatiently into the office and hurried her out to the studio. This time some of the students did not even bother to raise their cameras at her.

She went back to the dressing room and locked herself in. Then, still in costume, she sat down and smoked a cigaret. Since she had been told to take her time between changes, she would take plenty. Once she thought she heard the outside door open and then there was an exchange of voices, but the sound was so muffled that she could not hear more than a murmur. At last she snubbed out the cigaret butt and changed into the can-can outfit. This time it was the ties of the tights which were twisted and tangled and which had to be unsnarled before she could complete the change.

After she had put on the costume she decided to wait until she was called to go back to the studio. The rap on the door came more quickly than she expected.

The first person she saw in the studio was Bill, standing with a press-type camera and looking rather vacant. She opened her mouth to speak but an almost imperceptible shake of his head stopped her, and he turned away as though to ask technical advice of his neighbor.

Feeling as though a tremendous weight had been lifted from her shoulders, Cynthia arranged herself and watched Bill raise his camera along with the others. In a few moments he was filing through the door with the rest of the class.

She wasted little time in getting into the next costume, which was supposed to be Chinese and this time she did not wait in the dressing room. In the hallway she met Bill, who was coming toward her with an odd, angry expression.

"Get into the office," he said in a harsh voice which brooked no argument or discussion. "I'll be right back."

And, in a moment, he was, the cigar-chewing individual with him.

"Say, what is this?" the man with the cigar was protesting. "What is it you have to talk to me about? What's going on?"

"SHUT UP!" Bill roared, slamming the door behind them. He went directly to the phone and began to dial.

"Hey, that's a private phone! You can't barge in here like this and act like you was takin' over the place—"

Bill slammed the desk with his open palm. "SHUT UP, I SAID! I'm doing the talking. I have just dialed police headquarters ... "

"Police? Hey!" The man started for the phone, but checked himself as Bill half unwound himself from the chair.

"All but the last digit. I'm holding that until we see if you've got any sense at all." He turned to Cynthia. "I am now a registered student of the arts," he told her, "with all attendant rights and privileges—said privileges including the one of taking pictures through trick mirrors."

Cynthia gasped. "You mean those dressing room mirrors are—"

"They reflect on one side and can be seen through from the other. So, when these 'artists' can't get a model to pose nude willingly, they pursue their studies without her knowledge. I qualified as a fellow 'artist' by waving a camera and a five-dollar bill under the nose of the dean, here."

"Now looka here, we teach the est'etic part of the art game here, and it's people like you, who got no understanding of things like that who try to make it seem like somethin' else. Just because you're narrow-minded don't mean that the serious student gotta suffer—"

"I should hate to see you suffer," Bill said. "So listen carefully. I want you to bring each of those rah-rah boys in here for a little talk on the old college spirit. The talk will be brief. It will consist of me asking for the film he exposed tonight, after which you will show him to the door. The boys who are using film holders can get them back at my office, if they want to see me again. And don't try to pass off anything else on me. I want that film, and I'm going to get every bit of it. The first time I smell something phoney, I'll complete this call, and you can tell the whole story to a judge."

"Bill," Cynthia said. "I—I can't sit here and look at those men now. Not knowing that they ... "

"Right. Go back to the dressing room and wait. You can change, too, because our friend here is going to keep his students away from the mirrors and he is also going to put out most of the dressing room lights. O. K., Buster. Let's move."

Although Bill's apartment was only a few blocks uptown, and minutes away from the "art school", it was worlds apart from the grubby life which Cynthia had just glimpsed. Obviously a man's home, it was neither spotlessly immaculate nor suffering from slovenly neglect. There was a slight, casual disorder which indicated that in its tenant's interest, comfort, rather than military neatness came first. Nothing looked very new, and yet nothing was shabby. There were old ashes on the hearth, well-cured pipes on the mantel-piece. The leather bindings scattered here and there amongst the hundreds of books lining the walls were darkened and softened by much handling. In that place there was no over-polished gleam, but much of the deep, glowing patina which comes to things well used and undemonstratively cared for, and a faint incense of hickory smoke seemed to breathe from the rooms like a half-heard echo.

Cynthia sat in a deep armchair and watched Bill emptying film from his pockets onto a table.

"How in the devil" he demanded, "did you manage to get yourself into *that?*"

She explained, and he shook his head in mild, chiding reproof.

"You seem to have a special talent for getting mixed up in the wrong sort of situation," he said. "If it were someone else, I'd suspect that she was deliberately victimizing herself."

"Yes sir," said Cynthia, in such a mixture of real and mock meekness that his frowning disapproval was dispersed by a laugh.

"I want to make myself clear on one point," he said. "I know that photography, in the proper hands, can be an art form, and I know of several legitimate schools which include nude studies as one of the branches of that art. *One* of the branches, and, because it is a difficult and serious one, approached only after their students have been intensively grounded in the technique of handling the tools of their craft. I don't feel that I, myself, qualify as a photographic artist. I am, however, a good artisan, in the sense that some people are capable housebuilders if not inspired architects. And so, among other things, I have done a great many nudes, some of which I feel pretty good about. If you want to see what I'm talking about, you can look this over while I'm developing our friends' work." He pulled a portfolio from the shelves and laid it on the table beside her.

"You're going to ... develop those pictures?" Cynthia asked.

"Not if you object. But how else are you going to know that we have possession of all the pictures which were taken, that they won't turn up to haunt you someday as illustrations to some piece of under-the-counter erotica?"

"I hadn't thought of that possibility."

"You should, when you're dealing with little playmates like those."

Cynthia silently accepted a cigaret and turned it around and around in her fingers before lighting it.

"Bill," she finally said. "Bill, did you see me in the dressing room?"

"Yes. If you mean, do I know what you look like with your clothes off—I do."

"Then," she said in a tight voice, "I guess the negatives had better be developed."

She did not look at him, and, after a momentary hesitation, Bill gathered up the film and left the room.

While he was gone, Cynthia took up the book of photographs and studied it. And, studying it, she soon realized that, by Bill's definition, a naked shoulder and upper arm, the curving turn of a bare throat, was as much a nude as a full, unclothed figure. There were several of the latter, ranging in mood from the bright sparkle of a girl running along a shore to the shadowy, low-keyed brooding of a mature woman brushing her hair by candlelight. But, like flashing fragments of poetic imagery, like bits of remembered beauty to be caught and held in the mind's eye, were the dozens of broken, tender glimpses—the twisting arch of torso, the lifting reach of taut breasts, the ripe cradle of fecundity. Without understanding, or needing to understand, the technical devices by which the effects had been achieved, Cynthia sensed that through those pictures had been projected something which was a part of Bill. She was looking not only at the bodies of women, but into the heart of a man. And what she saw was—

"Well, that's done," Bill said.

Cynthia started slightly and closed the book, "So soon?"

"I rushed them through," he said. He was wiping his hands on a towel and he pursed his lips in pantomime request for a cigaret. Cynthia put one between his lips and lighted it. "They got all the care they deserve."

"May I see them?" Cynthia asked.

"You should, to check them. But you won't like them."

Cynthia followed him down a hall and into a midget-sized dark-room. Bill plunged his hands into a tank of fixing solution and dumped wads of negatives into a water bath.

"I've looked them over and they all seem to follow the same sequence," Bill said. "Taking into account double exposures and the fact that one kid I noticed didn't even know enough to take the cap off his lens, I think we have everything. But see for yourself."

Cynthia held a strip of film to the light. Even in negative there was something very unpretty in what she saw. Not satisfied with mere nudity, the "students" had evidently chosen their shots on the basis of complete revelation, with no other consideration in mind.

"Could you—would you make one quick print?" she asked. She chose a large, single negative which showed her in the ruffled pantaloons.

"Kicking yourself around?" Bill asked quietly.

"I have to know," she said. "It happened to *me*. I'd rather know what it was than imagine things."

Bill switched off the white light, closed the door, and in the murk of amber safe-lights wiped the wet negative and placed it in the enlarger. Within seconds he was rocking the paper in a tray, and Cynthia, watching over his shoulder, saw the faint outlines of a figure build into the image of herself. He tossed the print into a second tray, and in the unfamiliar half murk she stared at it.

"At least he was in focus," Bill said.

"Yes. He didn't blur anything," Cynthia said bitterly. "All right. I've seen all I need to."

"Watch!" Bill turned on the white light again. In front of Cynthia's eyes the print mottled, turned purple in parts, then fogged into complete black.

"I don't suppose you want these," he said, indicating the negatives. He poured a liquid into a tray, added water, and dropped the entire batch into the solution. "In five minutes they'll be blanks."

In the living room Cynthia forced herself to look into Bill's thoughtful eyes as he tamped tobacco into a pipe.

"I wonder what people say in a case like this?" she said. "I simply don't know how to go about thanking you for what you've done."

"It will be thanks enough," said Bill, if you'll just keep out of trouble in the future. Traditionally, of course, according to what I've learned from the movies, you're supposed to fall into my arms at this point."

"Oh," Cynthia said uneasily. He was holding his arms out and smiling now, mocking the attitude of a Hollywood hero. And, although he pretended to be joking, there was something half-expectant in his manner. A kiss, lightly given and without meaning, seemed small enough recompense for what he had done. And he could not know what effort even the most casual caress must be for her.

Trying to make it appear the friendly game he expected, she moved into the circle of his arms and turned her lips up to accept his. Their mouths met warmly and her body stiffened, protesting the intimacy. Her heartbeat quickened, and a hot flush spread through her body from a burning knot in the pit of her stomach. For only a moment she gave her mouth, and then her hands, which had been at her sides, were flat against his chest, pushing him away.

"Hey!" he protested. "That's not in the script!" He looked whimsically puzzled, but there was hurt disappointment in his manner as well.

"A—a button on my blouse bit me," she lied. Forcing herself, she put her arms about his neck and, with closed eyes, pressed her mouth again to his. She felt his lips' caress on hers, light as the stroking of bird's wing, then harder and more seeking as body molded to body, and torso knew torso intimately. Within her, the stir of an unfamiliar emotion questioned, like the face of a stranger, masked.

"Cynthia..." Bill's voice breathed in her ear, and still she rested in panic stillness in his arms, as a bird trembles in hand, fearful even of flight. The bone-carved strength of his cheek lay upon hers, his hand on the slim sculpture of her back drew her to him, the forward upthrust instinctive in her, and without knowledge. Emotion now the swelling tide of turbid sea, beating upon unknown walls of resistance, and again Bill's voice, "Cynthia..."

His fingers touched her arm, outlining the lyric swell as though tracing it into memory. Then her scant blouse, the warm palm cupping and eager on the silk. His lips again, touching upon her closed eyes and her cheeks, then flaming to her mouth.

"I didn't know," he said huskily. "I didn't know how much I wanted you."

He took a short step, as though to lead her to the couch before the fireplace, and with that movement, a spell was broken. Cynthia drew away, and when, not sensing her intent, he still held her, she twisted violently from him.

"Let me *go!*" she exclaimed.

He looked startled. Then chill masked his face, and he said quietly.

"Of course."

In the silence that followed, Cynthia pulled on her gloves.

"I don't want you to think I'm ungrateful for tonight," she said, turning. "I am terribly. But I'm disappointed to learn what you evidently expect in return. I thought you were—different. I'm especially disappointed because I didn't think you were the sort of person who'd be—excited—by a bunch of dirty pictures taken by nasty-minded Peeping Toms."

"I see. Well, if you feel that way about me I guess the best thing I can do is offer to drive you home."

"Thank you, but I can get a cab at the corner. And please try to understand. This is all very difficult for me, because I *am* grateful for your help tonight, and there are many things about you which I admire very much. It's just that I don't find this side of you very admirable, and I'd like to forget that I've seen it. I'd like to go on being friendly with you, and I think the easiest way to do that is just to pretend that part of tonight never happened."

"The part I'd like not to have happened," said Bill, "is the part that's happening now. To be perfectly honest, I suppose that seeing you posing tonight did have an effect on me. Among other things, I wanted to ask you to model for a new series of photos I've been thinking of doing. Now I see that you probably find that thought objectionable, and I can't very well defend it because I really don't know at what point Art, spelled with a capital, becomes simple voyeurism. If you're anti-sex, something like Rodin's 'The Kiss' must be pretty distressing. And, by the way, why *are* you against sex?"

"You're twisting everything around," Cynthia said. "You make me sound like a—like a blue-nosed reformer. And I'm not! I'm not! But there *must* be something besides sex! Why do people insist on bringing it up all the time? Why can't things be like ... like they are between Jan and me?"

"I don't know how things are between you and Jan Carter," Bill said. "I've wondered about that. And I'm wondering about something else. I'm wondering how you're going to explain to yourself your own sexual excitement of a few minutes ago." His voice acquired a bitter edge. "I, of course, was driven into a frenzy by the unaccustomed experience of looking at a pretty woman. Now, what about you?"

"*My* sexual excitement?" Cynthia gasped. "Are you trying to infer that when you kissed me I felt anything except—except disgust? Oh how little you understand! I feel sorry for you. I really do."

"I'm glad you can admit to feeling something, at any rate. I'd begun to think you were pretending *all* your emotions out of existence. If I were in the habit of giving advice, I would say that it's high time you stopped hypnotising yourself and your own feelings for a change. It's a lot more fun if you know what's going on."

"I don't see that there's anything to be gained by continuing this," Cynthia said. "We're just going to become more and more annoyed with each other. Thank you again for coming to—to rescue the maiden in distress. And let's try to continue to be friends, even if it seems difficult."

"I'm a pacifist myself," Bill said as he showed her to the door. "Sure I can't drive you? I smell rain in the air."

Cynthia managed a smile with her refusal, and said goodnight. Bill closed the door after her as she started down the two flights of stairs, then automatically reached into his pocket for the pipe which he had not finished filling.

"Bon jour, Mr. Hyde," he gravely greeted his reflected image in passing the hallway mirror.

He sat down in front of the fireplace, then, with the air of a man who has forgotten something important, rushed to a window and flung it open. Below, Cynthia had just gained the street. He shouted at her, and she looked up.

"I meant to tell you," he called. "I believe you're crazy as a coot, but I love you."

An old Italian man who was going by looked up and then nodded happily at Cynthia.

"That'sa nice," he approved. "That'sa very good." He beamed and opened his umbrella.

"Did you hear me?" Bill demanded in a roar. "I said—"

"She's hear you," the man yelled back. "By God, everybody's hear you!"

"All right, then," Bill said, and slammed the window.

CHAPTER ELEVEN

THE phone in Cynthia's apartment was ringing as she let herself in, and she hurried to answer it, frowning as she decided that it was probably Bill, checking to see that she had gotten home all right. But it was Jan, and the frown faded. She was in the neighborhood and was having trouble with her car.

"I'm calling from the garage now," she said. "They haven't even found the trouble yet, so I decided to call you and gossip away my boredom."

"Why not come over here and gossip?" Cynthia invited. "I want very much to have you see the place, now that it's finished. They can phone you here when the car is ready."

Jan accepted, and several minutes later Cynthia opened her door to her first, and rather damp, guest.

"It's coming down harder every minute," Jan complained as Cynthia hung her coat to dry. "A night to sit by the fire with a glass of port—which, incidentally I picked up to celebrate your house-warming."

She gave the bottle to Cynthia, and started on a keen-eyed tour of inspection. Touching a fabric here, now studying the effect of a lamp's placement, she was silent, save for an occasionally throaty murmur, half interrogation and half surprise, which might have meant anything. Cynthia tagged along in her wake, with a thousand self-deprecatory explanations on the tip of her tongue, waiting, with some apprehension for Jan's decision.

At last Jan was satisfied, and turned to her. Cynthia was by this time sure that Jan was displeased, and, despondent, she waited for the axe to fall. In that moment she could have broken to bits every stick of furniture, ripped every curtain and drape to shreds, so grotesque and awkward did they appear.

"It's perfect, Cynthia," Jan said. "You've made a lovely thing here."

And Cynthia bubbled over with happiness. A flood of trivial anecdotes and minor histories burst from her lips. Unbelievable bargains were again discovered; equally unbelievable attempts at fraud were exposed and scorned; such attendant difficulties as occurred when the kitten dabbled in the paint cans were reencountered and surmounted. And finally Jan, laughingly called a halt.

"Let's sit down and muse over it with our port," she suggested. "I'm being overwhelmed."

In the kitchen Cynthia struggled futilely with corkscrew and bottle.

"I can't draw the cork," she said. "Would you ... "

"I could, but I won't. This is your party, and I expect you to fulfill all attendant obligations."

Cynthia eventually returned with the bottle, two glasses, and bits of cheese and crackers on a painted tray.

"I broke the cork and had to push it in. Now we'll have to drink the whole bottle."

"Horrors! Well, here's to Cynthia's Sanctum."

"Should we have a fire?" Cynthia asked. "It's rather late in the season, but it *is* damp—and it seems appropriate to the occasion."

"Damper by the minute," Jan agreed. "It's really pouring now."

Soon a modest blaze was snapping briskly on the hearth, and, sitting next to Jan on the couch before it, Cynthia wondered briefly if another might now be crackling in Bill's place.

"The wine and the fire are doing things for you," Jan mentioned, after some talk concerned with the apartment. "When I came in I thought you looked rather dragged out."

"I got myself into another silly mess tonight," Cynthia told her. "It's so stupid that I'm ashamed to tell you about it."

"Then don't."

"But I want to."

"Then do. The atmosphere is so perfect for confidences that I'm almost tempted to talk about some of the silly things *I've* done. The night is turning so wild outside, and it's so snug here, that I feel completely isolated from the world."

And so Cynthia described her misadventure of that evening, telling the story slowly and in detail, with many reflective pauses as she sipped her port and refilled her glass and Jan's. The warmth from the fireplace seemed to intensify the glow which she soon began to feel as the effect of the wine stole subtly through her veins, with the result that inhibition slipped away, and any reticence which she may have felt was soon forgotten.

Jan at first quietly absorbed, grew markedly more restless as Cynthia described Bill's part in the incident. She twirled her glass rapidly between her fingers, lighted one cigaret from another and at last rose and began a measured pacing about the room.

"And then," Cynthia finished, "I took a cab home and found you on the phone."

Jan stood at a window and drew the curtain back, staring at the tracery of rain on the pane. Without looking around she said,

"And when he kissed you there was—nothing?"

"I was upset. And I was annoyed with myself for having led him to think that I might ... well, sleep with him."

"Cynthia, has it ever occurred to you that you might be—different from most women?"

"I don't know how most women are," Cynthia replied. "All I know is that I can't stand being pawed and handled that way."

Cynthia came and stood at Jan's side, and together they watched the rain sheeting across the deserted street below, shadows coming into sudden relief as chains of lightning forked viciously through the sky. Thunder rocked the night almost without pause and torrents poured down in a steadily increasing flood, voicing a toneless din.

"I'd better call the garage," Jan said. "It's getting late."

Her car, it developed, was not repaired, nor could it be that night.

"Have you a raincoat I could borrow?" she asked Cynthia. "I wouldn't dare take an umbrella out in this gale."

"You'll never flag a cab in this neighborhood tonight," Cynthia objected. "You'd better stay right here."

"It isn't too inviting out there," Jan admitted.

"Then I have my first overnight guest," Cynthia said.

"If it doesn't let up in half an hour," Jan amended.

Half an hour saw but a slight change in the weather, and that for the worse. It was, however, sufficient time for Cynthia to realize that her speech was becoming somewhat less exact and her laughter somewhat more unpredictable.

"Jan," she said with mock solemnity, "I think I am becoming an alcoholic. This is twice now that you've seen me like this."

"I don't think you have a problem there," Jan laughed. "What you need is a little more experience in gauging your capacity. But at the moment," she added, "what you appear to need more than anything is rest. You've worked harder than you realized in getting your apartment fixed up."

"We have a choice of two bedrooms," Cynthia said, "just as we have two living rooms and two dining rooms and two studies and two of whatever else you can think of except baths and kitchens. I've been sleeping in them by turns, because I don't know which I like better. But I think tonight I would like this one, because you can watch the lightning through the sky-light and when you get tired of the lightning you can watch the fire going out."

"This one by all means," Jan agreed, and together they began preparing the day-bed. The possibility of separate rooms was not suggested.

With the bed prepared, Cynthia went about the apartment on various small tidying chores, turning out lamps as she passed them until only one remained.

"We don't need this one either," Jan suggested, snapping it off also. "The firelight will be fine."

Naked skin glowed in soft tones of ruddy gold and shadowed, smokey amber as the two undressed.

"I hope you don't mind a kitten on your feet," Cynthia said. "This guy can't believe that I'm not his mother. He sneaks in and—"

Jan realized after a moment that the interruption was caused by something which Cynthia was staring at on the wall.

"It's ... our shadows," Cynthia replied to Jan's anxious question. "They remind me of ... the stable."

"Well, this *isn't* the stable," Jan said, briskly cross, "and you aren't going to spend the rest of your life afraid of your own shadow. Look here." She took Cynthia by the shoulders and turned her so that they faced each other, the sharp, dancing shadows now cast in profile. "Try to tell me your Jake had a profile like either of ours," she challenged.

Despite herself, Cynthia had to laugh. Things which she would have thought vulgar had anyone else expressed them, didn't seem so at all when they came from Jan. She bounced into bed and watched Jan's gold-outlined silhouette against the firelight as, back toward her, the older woman bent over some adjustment of her watch. If only Jan could be here always, she was thinking, to be with every night, to drive away the creeping loneliness that came so often ...

"I wish you lived here instead of my kitten," she said. "He's nice, but his conversation gets awfully dull."

"I might take you up on that," Jan said. "I'm no match for a kitten when it comes to bargaining, but we might strike a deal. A saucer of the very best cream every day?"

"No, it wouldn't be like that. We would just be here together and nobody would try to be the boss and everybody would be happy."

"I believe I've heard of a social institution which attempts to achieve at least part of that program. They call it marriage."

"Then let's get married. I can cook. I can sew. Every day I'd go shopping and come home with bundles and bundles of groceries and surprises for you."

"Comes the social revolution and perhaps we will," Jan promised. She sat on the edge of the bed and stared abstractedly into the fire. Cynthia slid one hand into hers, and she covered it warmly, strokingly.

"What are you thinking about, Jan?"

"You. Me. Us." She snapped her cigaret butt into the fireplace and moved in beside Cynthia.

"You're so warm," Cynthia purred. "But right now I see two of you." She blinked her eyes into focus, then sniffed at Jan's hair. "Last time we slept together you were wearing perfume. One of those sticky ones."

"I don't use—oh *that* night."

"I was so afraid that you wouldn't like this place. Compared to yours, it's a scooter next to a Rolls-Royce."

"My apartment is a pretty empty place sometimes, Cynthia."

The fire began to die, and as the room darkened, the skylight revealed more of the streaking fury which was raging across the night. Jan's fingers plucked the coverlet, and Cynthia was again aware of that almost-trembling tension when their bodies touched.

"Tell me about the rabbits, George..."

"What?" Cynthia asked puzzledly.

"Tell me about what it would be like. Tell us both some more of those pretty lies."

Cynthia nuzzled closer. "It would be like this, always. Nearness to someone who was good for you, and no angry thing could get in. We would laugh a lot, and I would write a letter to God asking to have an extra portion of sunshine to go with the way we felt. And we would lock the door and make faces at the stupid things that try to hurt."

A flash of lightning burst overhead, and in its tremulous flare Cynthia saw Jan's face, tight as though with pain, black eyes glaring upward in resentment against something unseen. She raised herself on one elbow, and her blonde hair spilled across Jan's shoulder.

"Jan." Anxiously. "What is it? What's the matter?"

"Nothing. Everything." She turned her face to the shadows, and Cynthia leaned over her.

"Jan, please don't. Is there something I can do?" Impulsively she put her lips to Jan's cheek and kissed her. Then she slid her arms around Jan and drew her near in an effort to comfort.

"Oh you little fool!" Jan whispered at her ear. "You lovable little fool!" Her mouth plunged to Cynthia's throat, then took her lips in demanding hunger. "God help you," she said, "God help us both."

The wind howled a lost, empty answer, and the last log on the hearth collapsed startlingly upon itself in a brilliant shower of sparks.

Long afterward, the room was still and silent, the fire fallen now wholly to ashes save for a coal or two which peered red-eyed out of the blackness. The storm had passed, and Cynthia, with a new knowledge in her eyes, stared sleeplessly at a dark sky which now and then flickered with a lessening electric blueness. From afar, thunder muttered like a snarling drum.

CHAPTER TWELVE

WAKING, Cynthia's first muddled thought was that she had overslept. Then she remembered that it was Saturday, and the events of the night rushed back to her mind. She was alone, and Jan had left a note:

I have an early appointment, and you looked so peaceful that I couldn't bear to wake you. And perhaps it's better for you to be by yourself while you decide what last night really meant to you and what you are going to do about it. Whatever you decide, Jan loves you.

Loves me, Cynthia thought. Bill, shouting out a window. Jan writing me a note. And what they both mean . . .

She decided to shower before breakfast. In the bathroom, while she waited for the water to run warm, she met her naked self in the paneled mirror of the door. She studied her body and her face. The eyes which looked back into hers were as candidly clear as ever, her healthy freshness unchanged.

"What did you expect to find?" she mocked herself. "A scarlet description of your sins tattooed on your middle?"

This, then, was the face which had turned from Bill's kiss to seek Jan's; this the body she had withheld from him in fierce anger, only to sacrifice it on the altar of a perverse passion. Willingly, though at times uncertain, she had given herself up to every strange, unnatural demand of Jan's abnormal nature, and no detail of her abandonment to that anomalous love-making was less than needle-sharp in her memory. These the breasts on which Jan's head had lain; this the path her warm wet mouth had followed; these thighs knew her strength and seeking gentleness.

"You little fool!" she exclaimed, unconsciously paraphrasing Jan's words. "You fraudulent little fool!" Her lips formed a word she had never spoken, and she watched her mouth curl over the obscene curtness of it. She thought of another word, and used that, and then she voiced every lewd and offensive phrase she had ever heard. And still the mirrored figure smiled with apparently ingenuous frankness.

She had just stepped from her bath when the phone rang. Wrapping herself in a towel, she answered it and recognized Bill.

"Good morning," he said. "Are we friends today?"

"I couldn't blame you if we weren't. I was pretty unpleasant last night. Would it help if I said I was upset?"

"Huh?" Bill grunted as though jolted heavily. "What?"

"I'm trying to apologize for my ill-mannered display of surliness."

Silence, and then Bill said.

"I wish they'd hurry up with video-phones. If I could see your face, maybe I'd know just how much of this is a rib."

"A video-phone," said Cynthia, "would reveal several ribs. I am sitting here in a towel which doesn't know how to be a sarong. Tell me, is it sarong to wear a sarong when answering a video call?"

Bill groaned. "There is always the possibility that it's sarong number," he suggested.

"I might have known that you would skirt the entire subject.

"Have you been putting little white pills in your coffee?" Bill asked suspiciously.

"I haven't had my coffee yet. Just got up."

"Well, while you're having it you might decide whether or not you want to work today. The green light just flashed on that catalogue job."

"I can tell you right now. Yes. What time? An hour from now?"

"Will that be convenient for your *duenna?*"

"Jan won't be with me. If those clothespin tucks require a woman's touch, I'm afraid you'll have to find one."

"I think I can manage alone," Bill said. "And I think I will hang up right now, before you wake up and change your mind."

And he did.

Some time later, as she walked to Washington Square Park for her bus, Cynthia noticed something of which she had never before been aware. It was not only lounging groups of candy-store Casanovas, not alone the older, bullish men who seemed always to be picking their teeth in doorways as she passed, not only the finicky-neat clerk-types who hastened nervously as though pursued by time—not just these whose eyes obviously speculated as she went by. There were women, too, whose appraisal contained more than the unconscious, critical, estimation accorded a potential rival in a vast sexual competition. Women in whose manner she thought she detected something that was a part of Jan. They were not many—no more than a handful of the hundreds of people she passed—but to Cynthia they assumed an exaggerated importance.

She wondered whether she was inventing a situation out of a guilty conscience, or whether her experience had simply opened her eyes to something which had been there all the time. Or was there something in her manner, now, which gave her away to women of that type? In her mirror she had looked in vain for some sign which would hint at the enormity of that vicious knowledge which was now hers. Still, she had read somewhere that drug-addicts were almost inhumanly able to recognize fellow victims, and it might follow that any abnormality developed a high sensitivity to symptoms of vice in others.

In at least one instance, the latter possibility appeared likely. A big-boned woman in horsey tweeds was walking her dachshund in the park as Cynthia passed through, and she turned to stare openly at Cynthia's approaching figure. On her face was such an obvious question that Cynthia confusedly lowered her eyes and blushed. A chiding finger wagged, and a voice which was both amused and knowing murmured,

"Naughty. Very naughty, little rabbit."

Cynthia hurried a bit faster.

On arriving at Bill's office, Cynthia found him engaged in a spirited technical discussion with one of the oddest-looking men she had ever seen. Almost as tall as Bill, but round as a barrel, he looked like nothing so much as a trained bear. His clothing hung in voluminous, unpressed folds, his mop of reddish hair started out in all directions and arrived nowhere. Beneath bushy brows his eyes popped fiercely, and from his upper lips sprouted a tremendous, silky moustache of such comic design that Cynthia at first suspected it of being false—especially since it was black. He carried an outrageously large walking stick with a gold knob, and this he used alternately as a resting place for his chin and as a weapon with which to pound the floor as he drove home some point of argument.

This, Cynthia soon learned, was Hans Schlagel, a name she recognized as that of the most famous commercial photographer in the country.

"My favorite model," Bill introduced her. "Isn't she lovely? And smart, too. Say something clever, Cynthia."

"Hello," Cynthia offered.

"See? No effort at all. It just comes natural to her."

"I do not much care for intellectual women," Schlagel growled. "A model's business is to be beautiful."

"*And* to make money," Bill reminded. "Ah, the pretty, pretty monies! It makes me feel warm all over just to think about it."

"Enough of these business details. When can I photograph her?"

"Ah, you weel take zee wonairful peekchair, no?"

"I weel take zee poke at your nose in a minute. I can use her for a *Journal* cover, maybe."

Cynthia's heart began to bounce. A cover by Schlagel was the sort of thing models dreamed of, plotted after, remembered to mention in their prayers. But Bill was saying—

"You can't have her. She has no time. Her services are in great demand."

"What *are* you spouting off about? She's here, isn't she?"

"As a personal favor to an old dear friend. I swear she's busy all next week. Yes, and the week after." He winked at Cynthia and nodded significantly toward the House of Cimier.

"Is this true?" the great man demanded sternly of Cynthia.

"Why—yes. Yes, I'm quite busy."

The gold-headed cane banged explosively on the floor. Schlagel walked around and around the girl, studying her from all angles, and his face grew blacker with each revolution. Now that it seemed he would be unable to hire her, it grew more and more necessary that he should. Bill winked again and leaned back, twiddling his thumbs.

"I'll buy off your appointment," Schlagel finally suggested.

"You will not. You'll stand in line like everybody else. Unless—no, you wouldn't want to do that."

"Unless what? Stop mumbling, man."

"Oh, I was going to suggest that you could use my studio for a few minutes right now. But you wouldn't want to use my stuff. It's all held together with rubber bands and scotch tape."

Rap of the stick, and a glower.

"I have sold pictures, youngster, made through a pin-hole in an oatmeal box, and from what I know of it, your equipment is only slightly more primitive. Come, young lady. We have work to do."

"This is going to cost you," Bill warned. "Not the usual cut-rate price you try to pay."

"You bother me. Go across to the florist's and buy flowers. Lots of flowers. And we will want a basket to put them in."

An hour later Schlagel stomped out of the studio with a parcel of exposed film under his arm and a satisfied, Cheshire-cat smirk on his broad face. Bill grinned after him.

"Happy as a lark," he said. "You'd think he'd just cornered the market in wheat."

"You cheated," Cynthia accused. "You made him think I was the town's most popular model."

"I didn't cheat him. I steered him into a good thing. And you *will* be deluged with offers when that cover appears. Right then you'll have to decide whether you're going to model seriously or stay on your present job. That's how good he is."

"I think *you're* good. When do we get to work?"

"After you've rested," Bill laughed. "Sit down and take it easy. I'll go for coffee."

Afterward he showed her the dresses she was to model, and left her in the dressing-room while he arranged his sets.

The first garment she put on was not only overly large, but was a style and cut unlike anything she had ever worn. Then the garment's purpose dawned on her, and she laughed aloud.

"Bill," she called. "Look at this."

He came into the dressing-room, took one look, and struck his forehead.

"Good lord, how did a maternity dress get into this? No. Take it off. You don't suit it."

"Nobody will. It's a stupid design. I've got it hooked, but I can't unhook it."

Bill slipped the fasteners for her, and began to look over the other garments.

"You can have this back," Cynthia said coolly.

He turned, and she was in her panties and bra, holding the dress toward him.

"Excuse me," he said. "I thought this was the Grand Central waiting room."

"You've seen me in less than this."

"Yes, I have, but—Pardon me if I seem confused. I *am* confused. I can't figure you out."

"Don't worry, neither can I. And I make it a fulltime job. Would you give me something else to put on, please?"

He helped her on with a dress, took a tuck here and there, and checked it carefully for wrinkles.

"This is somewhat unorthodox, you know," he said. "Not at all the approved relationship between photographer and model."

"Then let's be completely unorthodox. I think I would like you to kiss me, if you will, please."

Moving into his arms, she turned her face up to his, grasping his lapels in her fists and raising herself on tiptoe.

"Miracles are happening today," he said wonderingly. "It will rain frogs by nightfall."

His lips tentatively touched hers, and he found her kissing him back. He kissed her harder then, and still she kissed him.

"Thank you," she said. "That will do nicely for the present."

He loosened his tie and said,

"I don't mind being used a little, but I can't help a bit of curiosity. Did you find out what you wanted to know?"

"How did you know I was trying to find out something?"

"I didn't. I'm shooting in the dark."

"So am I. I think we'll have to try it again sometime."

"I'll be looking forward to it."

They went on with their work, and time slipped away. It was early afternoon when Bill switched off his lights, covered his camera against dust, and mopped his brow with a handkerchief already damp.

"That does it," he sighed. "I didn't expect to overwork you this way, but I didn't know Schlagel would drop in. You won't regret the time you gave him, though."

"I'm not at all tired," Cynthia said. "You're forgetting that I spend most of my time in a gymnasium."

She went back to the dressing-room and removed the last outfit she had modeled. With her hand on the hanger which held her own street clothes, she paused. She sat down and lighted a cigaret, and after she had taken a few nervous puffs, she took off her brassiere. She smoked for a few minutes more, started to put the brassiere back on, and laid it down again.

"Are you about ready for lunch?" Bill yelled from somewhere.

"Just a minute," she called back.

She took a last, gasping drag on her cigaret, and then wrenched it to shreds in an ashtray. Swiftly, then, standing before a mirror, she ran a comb through her hair. Her hands were trembling when she sat down.

"Bill," she called in a voice which might have been steadier. "Would you come in a minute?"

He stopped at the doorway.

"Yes," she said. "I want you to come in."

He advanced with the air of one who expects the ground to open beneath his feet.

"If you think I'm crazy, I won't blame you," she said. "But I can't bear to have you remembering me like—like those pictures those degenerates took of me. This is how I want you to think of me, not the way it was in that five-dollar-a-peek place. I want you to look at me, and I want to see your face when you look at me. I know you weren't willingly spying, I don't want to carry around that kind of a memory. This is I, and you can look as hard and as long as you want to. No charge, without the trick mirrors."

"You are very lovely," Bill said simply. "You have a mole I didn't know about."

"Very few others know about it. And Bill—you said something about wanting to take some nudes of me. If you want to, we can start now. I'm really not tired."

"You may not be—I am," Bill replied. "I'll put the offer on file, and if you still feel the same way in a few days from now, we'll do something about it. Frankly, I think that something is driving you into a peculiar, almost hysterical state where you're likely to say things and do things which you may regret tomorrow morning. I'm not going to stick my nose into your business beyond saying that a change of atmosphere might help. The circus is in town and I promised a kid down in my neighborhood that I'd take him. How about it?"

"Oh, fine," Cynthia said. "And just to show you how gracefully I can accept rejection, I'm going to have a wonderful time. After all, when it's a choice between a naked girl and a circus—well, everybody loves a circus."

"And you can eat peanuts at the circus—"

"Without hating yourself in the morning. And now, if you'll excuse me, I'd like to get dressed, and that is a very private matter."

CHAPTER THIRTEEN

JAN CARTER flipped the bulky envelope onto the massive, efficiently bare desk. She pulled off her hat and dropped it on a chair.

It was pay-off time. That was one thing about Jan, she was always prompt to pay her debts. Besides, she wanted to be under the least possible obligation to this creature who sat behind the desk—this man who pulled all sorts of strange strings. Had meeting him been a stroke of good or ill fortune, Jan asked herself. After all, her association with him had brought her if not wealth, then comfort—security, if you wanted to call it that—and, above all, ample opportunity to indulge her difficult idiosyncrasy. Around her, day after day, were women—lots of women, all sorts of women. Tall and short, young and middle-aged, fair and dark, women of every type, every background, every aspect. A man in her shoes, she knew, would consider himself fortunate indeed; and after all, despite her bountiful womanly charms she was herself something of a man. Why then should she have misgivings about this silent partner, about the enterprise she operated with his connivance? She tapped the bulky envelope with her manicured forefinger.

"I think you'll find that correct," she said over her shoulder. Tossing her head to shake out her hair, she pulled a chair near the corner of the desk and sat down.

The ruggedly handsome and middle-aged face of the man lit up in that expansive, confidence-inspiring smile long familiar to millions of strap-hanging newspaper readers. His china-blue eyes twinkled behind their pince-nez like those of a benign Santa Claus as he casually dropped the envelope into a drawer.

"I don't need to count it," he said. "I have every confidence in your honesty, especially since it is augmented by an almost masculine good sense."

"I suppose that is intended as a compliment," Jan said, waving away a cigaret he offered and taking one of her own, "so I will thank you. However, I simply don't think it would be smart tactics for me to attempt cheating my—my business associate."

"And you are quite right. Were you to act otherwise, I fear that your, ah, weight-reducing enterprise would soon run into grave difficulties."

"Speaking of difficulties, what about that woman detective I mentioned a few weeks ago? I smelled police as soon as she walked in."

"I checked on that. You were right, of course. Merely a matter of overzealousness on her part, ah, ignorance on the part of her superior. She has been transferred."

"She shouldn't have been around in the first place. It makes me nervous, and I don't like it."

"Now, now, let's not get excited. A few of your, ah, clients are bound to gossip now and then, with the result that some minor official becomes curious. You're not bothered very often, are you?"

"Once is too often. My part of the job is to run the place as quietly and efficiently as possible. I don't know whether or not you think it important, but we haven't had a fatality. And your job, as I understand it, is to see that I'm not interfered with, not merely to receive me here once a month and collect a piece of the profits."

The smile flickered, then steadied.

"Let us review our relative positions," the man said. "As I recall it, I merely invested heavily in a business you wished to enter—an enterprise which you call, for some whimsical reason, the House of Cimier. In my connection as a silent partner, I have no direct contact with the business, and have never even been on the premises. I do receive a certain return on my investment, and further than that I know nothing. Any, ah, irregularities which might exist there would come as a complete and outrageous shock to me."

"So I'm left holding the bag if there's trouble."

"If by 'holding the bag' you mean that you are obliged to rely on my private promise to see that you are not investigated—yes. However, you know that my word is good, and so long as I remain in the political picture, believe me, you have nothing to worry about on that score."

"Suppose we just talk straight for a minute," Jan said annoyedly. "Two and a half years ago you were in the middle of a hot election fight, with the reform party out for your hide. They couldn't get a thing on you—and then suddenly one of these high-school girls you like to educate turned up pregnant, stubborn, and ready to kill herself. I don't suppose you'd have minded if she did, but she was hysterical and wanted to shout her story from the housetops."

"And then you stepped in," the man prompted politely.

"And then I stepped in, because I happened to know her sister. And I found out what the sister couldn't. I came to you. By that time I had gained her confidence to such an extent that I was sure she'd do whatever I said—and that confidence was something you'd have given a million for, just then. But my price wasn't a million."

"You could have done better than you did," the man admitted.

"I didn't come to you to get a thing for myself, and you know it damned well. All I asked for was a decent break for that girl. A good doctor and enough money to give her two years art study in Europe, where she might have a chance to forget some of the things you'd taught her. It was you who originally suggested our own—business association, after pointing out that there are plenty of wealthy women ready to pay almost any price for the sort of service our Dr. Ramsey now performs."

"I found that a necessity. Obviously you had not come to blackmail me yourself, and your demands for the girl were extremely moderate. But, with the knowledge you had, you could still be dangerous. What was more logical than to maneuver you into check by urging you into an enterprise which was, ah, slightly illegal? It was a very good form of insurance, since it not only, ah, spiked your guns, but made a profitable investment as well. I should have been greatly disappointed had you been adamant, but with the possibility of quick riches pointed out to you, it was ludicrously easy to overcome your scruples against breaking a law which is both civil and natural."

"Don't over-rate my scruples. You see, I have very little sympathy with your 'natural law' which in so many cases places the whole responsibility on the woman while the man escapes scot-free. Take that girl who was with us last week. Three months before her debut was scheduled, she had her first drink, and then several more, at a wild party. Passed out, and hadn't any way of knowing which of several boys might have been the child's father. Or there's Mrs. Kade, whose husband is known to be impotent. What was she to do when the man responsible took off like a jet—claim a miracle?"

"We can do without the argumentative lecture. I find it as boring as unconvincing."

"Very well. You entered this business just as deeply as I did. You provided the money and agreed to see that it was protected. Our first customers were friends of your friends, although I am sure that your connection was unknown to them. Yet now you are beginning to act as though we weren't in this thing together. A few minutes ago you said that I have nothing on which to rely except your private promise. I have more than that, and if you fail to live up to your part of the bargain, I can still use it."

"May I ask what that is?"

"The story of the girl who could have ruined you. Obviously I'm not going to use it unless I find you trying to leave me in a jam. But I want you to know that under extreme circumstances, I *will* use it. Perhaps that knowledge will make you a bit less casual about maintaining your part of the bargain."

"In other words, if you go down, I go down with you."

"That's right. A mild form of justifiable blackmail."

The smile faded so slowly that one could not have said when it disappeared, and the eyes which had twinkled now glinted like flint.

"I think the time has come for us to reorganize," the man said. "You should know by now that I never enter a situation in a subordinate position. I like being the boss, and I have not enjoyed our association as it previously stood. As of now, I should like you to realize that *I am the boss.* Evidently you did not read yesterday's papers very thoroughly. The girl of whom you speak was killed in a plane crash in Florida."

Aside from a flickering twist of her mouth, Jan gave no sign of shock. She studied the glow of her cigaret as a poker player studies a bad hand. Then, as though tossing the hand into discard, she said,

"I guess that changes things a bit."

"Considerably. Since I have never had any contact with Dr. Ramsey, the only link which could connect me with such a scandal is now broken, and your threat is quite empty. On the other hand, I need only turn to my phone to set in motion the machinery which would result in a raid, your arrest, and a lengthy prison sentence imposed by a judge of my selection. Any counter-accusation you might make would be of negligible consequence. I am continually being attacked by disgruntled cranks who can produce no evidence."

"It was very stupid of me to trust you."

"Not really. You have never known me to go back on my word, and I have no intention of breaking off our relationship, for I find the investment one of my most profitable. But from now on I want you to understand who is in the driver's seat. And I think I shall enjoy driving you. Oh, I shan't use the whip. Just a flick now and again to remind you it's there. But it's high time you were broken to harness. Your pleasure in your independence has been most unseemly."

"You are so horrible," Jan said calmly, "that you're fascinating. I know of your sexual sadism, of course—you've been quite open about that. But I didn't realize that it went so far afield. I thought your brutalities were confined to the bedroom."

"I have never made any effort to disguise my hatred of women. In a manner of speaking, my dear Jan, we are opposite sides of the same coin."

"Not quite. I don't dream of torturing men; I just like women better. And I didn't know that you considered me a woman."

"Since we are discussing our aberrations," he said, "let me say that I believe I could enjoy someone like you much more than I could enjoy a normal woman—simply because I know you would hate every minute of it."

"I see—it's no fun for you if it's fun for the woman, is that it?"

"Precisely. And that is why I did not care for that woman you introduced me to recently, that actress."

"My mistake. Among other failings, I seem to be a poor panderess. After watching her enjoying our masseur's maulings, I thought you were made for each other."

"Not at all. She liked it. A disgusting creature."

"Well, Mr. Boss-Man," Jan said, "I don't like the new look of this thing. Suppose I just decide to sell out?"

"What have you to sell? Apparently the, ah, the House of Cimier is a very profitable concern, but any prospective buyer would immediately find a discrepancy between your falsified books and the actual, legitimate volume of business. Of course you could simply close up and sell your equity in the property if you can find a buyer for such a monstrosity. My personal feeling is that you would find yourself bankrupt—as well as in jail. For at the first sign of any irregularity, I should, of course, consider our agreement null and void, and do my utmost to see that the ends of justice were well served."

"I see. I can't get out if I want to."

"Oh, I wouldn't say that. Possibly at some future time, we might come to some agreement, if that seemed mutually advantageous. Of course it would involve a large cash settlement on your part—but you had nothing when you started, so it should not inconvenience you too much to find yourself penniless."

"Remind me not to vote for you, next election. Anything else?"

"Not now. Oh, before you go—in driving by the place I have twice noticed a very striking young blonde girl coming out." And he described Cynthia.

"That's Cynthia Bennett. I hired her recently."

"I want to meet her."

"You want to meet *her*? What in the world for? Or is that a stupid question?"

"From you, yes." He explained, very bluntly, exactly why he wanted to meet her.

Jan's eyes widened in distaste. Then she shook her head.

"No. Not Cynthia. Sorry."

Little bunches of muscle stood out on the close-shaven cheeks as the man's jaw set.

"And why not?"

"She's not for you. She's an innocent, bewildered kid from East Jalopy or someplace. Nothing like that is going to happen to her if I can help it."

"I find this very interesting. I am not asking you to tie her up in a bag and have her delivered here. I said that I wanted to meet her."

"And we both know what that means. She'd be terribly impressed at meeting the Big Shot. There'd be an intimate little dinner here, with too much to drink. And then, when she was still reluctant, there'd be another, very special, drink. Oh, I've heard about those very special drinks you sometimes make. Then, for the next day or so, you wouldn't be at home, and nobody would know where she was. Or perhaps, if you felt like it, you'd let her come to the phone, and she'd insist that she was having a wonderful time as your house-guest, talking with a crazy giggle that would stay with her until the dope wore off. No. You aren't going to do that to her."

"Very noble sentiments, I must say. Yet only a few weeks ago..."

"Only a few weeks ago I introduced you to a Broadway actress whom you knew to be taking one of my courses. A woman at least as depraved as you are, who wanted to know you for your influence and didn't care what she had to do to get it. But I am not, aside from that lapse, your procuress, and if I were, I would certainly do all I could to keep your dirty paws off a girl like Cynthia."

"This," said the man, "seems to be the showdown. I have just gone to some lengths to explain who is running things now. I want to meet this Cynthia, and I intend that you shall introduce us. In fact, I shall insist that you bring her here tonight."

"I won't do it."

"You will. Right now we are going to establish, once and for all, that you are taking orders from me. I am completely out of patience with your attitude, and I warn you that I am ready to conclude this situation at once. I have been careful to keep a check on some of your, ah, irregular clients. A little pressure, the threat of scandal, and they will quickly turn against you. Dr. Ramsey will too, if she's offered immunity in exchange for testimony. You know that I do not bluff."

"The Big House for me, eh?"

"Undoubtedly. Rather a high price to pay for the—honor—of some moppet you are evidently trying to keep to yourself."

"And all this just to show me who's boss?"

"It appears that you have some difficulty in learning."

"I'm afraid I can't learn. If it's a choice between turning that girl over to you and taking my chances in court, I'll take the latter."

"You speak as though going to bed with a man were like buying a one-way ticket to hell."

"With you, it must be."

"You have, of course, been to bed with men?"

"One. Just once. He meant well, I think, but it made me sick. I can't think of anything worse than being with someone like you. And before I'd let Cynthia in for that, I'd—I'd go to bed with you myself!"

He had been sitting forward tensely on his chair. Now he leaned back, and a thoughtful half-smile reappeared.

"Do you know," he said, "that might be very entertaining. Actually, as you must realize, I could very easily meet the girl through other channels—if she were my main interest. The issue is really to determine your subordination to me—and your last suggestion offers vast possibilities. *Vast* possibilities."

Jan watched him as she might have watched a coiled serpent, saying nothing. He leaned his classic head sideways, the better to look at her slim legs.

"You have, in effect, made two counter propositions to my suggestion that you arrange a meeting between this girl and me, the first being that you go to jail and the second being that you accept my love. I feel that the second alternative offers more advantages to both of us, and I am willing to accept that as payment in full for your refusal. Let us say, then, that you will remain here this evening and I will forget that there is such a girl as this Cynthia of yours."

Jan's voice was streaked with hatred and revulsion.

"You swine!" she exclaimed. "You filthy-minded, nauseating beast!"

"Exactly. I am glad that you have that approach—it will be so much more charming when you consider your own status in catering to one of whom you have such an opinion."

"I think you had better start your arrangements for putting me in prison," Jan said stonily.

"Ah, but what then of your dear little Cynthia? Isn't it possible that she might be persuaded that by, shall we say, being nice to me she might influence me to interest myself in obtaining your freedom? Not that I *would* be influenced, you understand ... but she needn't know that for some time."

"You wouldn't!" Jan exclaimed. But she sounded uncertain.

"You know that I would. For simple revenge, which I make no pretense of concealing. I think I should enjoy thinking of you in prison, knowing you were helpless to make any move, wondering when—*exactly* when—your little friend would be ... persuaded. Perhaps I should send you word, now and then, of her latest, ah, progress. You see, my imagination runs rather to the old-fashioned, but still effective, villainies."

Twice Jan started to speak, then broke off. On the third attempt she said:

"There just aren't words. They haven't invented words to describe what I feel at this minute."

"Then we shan't be overburdened with senseless expressions of amazement. In a moment I shall retire to my bedroom to make a change of clothing. But first, I should like to have yours, so that I can take them with me. In case you should later decide to change your mind, you see, and try to leave."

She shuddered, and the man smiled.

"I believe, my dear Jan, that at last I have you cornered. A strange weakness, this feeling you have for that girl."

"If I—if I go through with this," Jan said, "I want one thing clearly understood. You agree to leave the girl alone? Absolutely, and for always?"

"Will you accept my word?"

"Yes."

"I will display no further interest in her. I have never broken a promise."

"No, you're an Eagle Scout."

"I should advise you not to be flippant. And I am waiting for your clothes."

"You want me to undress here? In the study? And go running around the house naked?"

"You know I dismiss the servants before receiving, ah, business associates. We will not be disturbed. I am waiting."

Slowly Jan unbuttoned her jacket and laid it aside. Her eyes, contemptuous and bitter, bored into the man's—and he stared back unwaveringly. She took off her blouse next, and unzipped her skirt. The man leaned forward slightly, and the tip of his tongue slipped across his lips. Her slip crackled electrically in the quietness of the room as it went over her head. In bra and panties, stockings and shoes, she stood while the man eyed her body with a kind of cynical amusement.

"Before I go any further," she said, "may I have one of those very special drinks you make? I'm not sure that I can get through this if I know what I'm doing."

"Certainly. I'll get it now." He picked up the clothing she had removed, saying, "The rest can wait. I hardly think you'll leave the house in your present lack of dress."

He left her alone, and for several minutes Jan paced the richly carpeted floor like a caged feline. She had an impulse to pick up the phone and try to call Cynthia, to tell her that whatever happened, she was under no circumstances to have anything to do with ... *him*. But it seemed a worrisome and probably useless cruelty to bewilder the girl with what must seem a fantastic request—particularly so since its motivation must remain secret. No, the best thing to do was simply pay off, accept her bitter medicine. He was, after all, a man of his word.

She was standing with her back to the door, unseeingly studying a family portrait, when he returned. She heard him set down a glass, heard him clear his throat. Then she turned. The sight that met her eyes was so unexpected and bizarre that she drew back in amazement. The thought came to her that he was showing off a costume intended for masquerade.

"What—what *is* it?" she gasped.

"It's my Superman suit," he said with testy dignity. He expanded his chest and adjusted his pince-nez. His waist, at which an air pistol was slung on a massive leather holster, was so unnaturally constricted that she knew he was wearing a reducing corset. The entire effect was so ridiculous that she was suddenly convulsed with over-wrought laughter.

It seemed even funnier when she watched him slip the revolver from its holster and turn it in her direction. There was a snapping "paff!" and a leaden pellet stung her thigh, then rattled against the wall. The laughter choked in her throat.

"Don't laugh at me," he said in a voice from which all pretence of suavity had vanished. "Whatever you do, don't laugh at me."

A chill of horror needled into Jan's spine as she saw the air pistol swing upward with careful aim until it centered at her eyes.

"Don't laugh at me," he repeated.

"No," Jan said. "No."

"Now take off the rest of your clothes."

The lesson had begun.

CHAPTER FOURTEEN

O N Monday morning when Cynthia arrived at work, she
found that Jan, usually punctual, had not yet appeared.
She herself was late, having unconsciously contrived a series of
those procrastinating delays by which the individual commonly
reveals his reluctance to face a distasteful situation. After the
events of their last night together, Cynthia had anticipated their
next meeting with less and less enthusiasm.

For, how could she face Jan now? she had wondered. The
things which had passed between them were of such a nature
that it seemed unlikely that they could now approach each other
with anything but an uneasy embarrassment. And Jan's note had
indicated that she more or less expected Cynthia to make some
sort of a considered decision concerning their future relationship. Indicated, in a way, that she hoped that evenings like that
last one would become a regular part of their lives.

Cynthia tried to analyze herself, tried to read deeply not only
into her own mind but into her inmost feelings; she knew that her
future happiness, her whole life, were at stake in the decision she
must now reach. What, for instance, was her real feeling for men
generally, and for Bill in particular? Had her past truly ruined
her for male companionship? Was she twisted beyond recovery,
especially now that she had tasted the forbidden fruit—the solace
of communion with another woman?

A great many things were clear to her, now that the first
shock of that experience had passed. She had known, of course,
that there were Lesbian women, women whose affection was

given to others of their own sex, women whose sex urges were so warped that normal masculine love was denied them. Yet, in her lack of experience, she had never once connected that term with Jan Carter, or any other woman of her acquaintance. She had thought of Lesbians somewhat as she thought of the duck-billed platypus—strange creatures both, whose existence was known, but who were seldom encountered. Now she understood that not only was Jan a complete invert, but that her own friendship with Jan had been the subject of considerable outside speculation. Bill, had wondered about it, and had been almost open in explaining his antagonism toward Jan on those grounds. Chance remarks amongst the girls with whom she worked were now recalled with a new meaning. And Meg, it was obvious, was truly and overtly jealous. It was quite possible, Cynthia supposed, than Jan had also had an earlier affair with Meg. Quite calmly she tried to analyze her feeling toward Meg, and to herself admitted that she returned Meg's antagonism. Was this an abnormal jealousy on her part, or was it merely a normal defense against Meg's habitual unpleasantness?

She could not say, for the one thing which was far from clear was her own self. Was she too, a Lesbian, or had she only been weak, too grateful for Jan's affectionate understanding to rebel at the price of that affection? Did she truly hate all sex, as she had believed, or was it only men whom she found repellent? In Jan's embrace, she had to remember, she had found—release. Could she find that release with the only man in whose presence she felt any similar companionship ... Bill? And how important were the other things to her, the things which two women together could never have—children, a lasting home?

She was not ready to answer those questions, and she was glad that Jan was not there to ask them, if only with her presence. She hurried through the office, but not before Meg, with a problem that evidently required Jan's attention, stopped her to ask, coldly,

"Will Miss Carter be in soon?"

"I haven't the slightest idea."

"Oh? I thought you were probably together, since you're both late."

Cynthia passed on without further comment. Some time later she heard that Jan had called to say she was ill and would not be in for a day or two.

During the rest of the morning, the problem of what course to take in her dealings with Jan occupied much of her time, and at noon she decided to phone. If Jan needed her, she would be there, and if not—well, it was easier to speak to her over a wire than to talk to her face to face.

The phone rang a long time when she dialed, and she was about to hang up when Jan's voice, thick and sleepy, answered. She was glad that Cynthia had called, Jan said, but she did not sound glad. She sounded terribly tired, and disjointed, with long pauses between phrases, and once or twice she forgot altogether what she had been saying. But Cynthia gathered that she felt herself to be not seriously ill, and that she preferred being alone and resting to having callers. What she needed most, she said, was sleep.

"You sound as though you've had too many sleeping pills already," Cynthia said, only half jesting.

"Do I? Well, I'll be careful. And I'll be a new woman when you next see me."

But when she returned to work two days later, she was far from her usual, buoyant self. Her skin looked drawn and yellow, and her walk was without springiness. She seemed abstracted and forgetful, and she spent a great deal of time in her office. It was several days before she recovered her normal, healthy appearance and cheerfulness, and even then the recovery of her spirit lagged. During those days Cynthia saw her infrequently, for Jan took to arriving at work somewhat later than usual and leaving earlier. No mention was made of the subject which had been uppermost in Cynthia's mind, and for the present she was satisfied to let the situation remain so.

At the same time, Cynthia began seeing Bill more often. During the two weeks which followed, she was often glad to find herself in his company, to be amused by the rapid flash of his apparently effortless wit, beneath which, she had come to understand, a firm, yet relaxed assurance of purpose lay. Further assignments in which he could find a place for her had come in, and on several evenings they worked together in his studio, later going out for coffee or an occasional high-ball before he drove her home. On weekends, too, they found themselves together as Bill arranged his schedule to fit her free hours, and there were stolen periods of truancy also, when work was set aside in favor of the more attractive beguilements of the art museums or theatres. Once or twice Bill told her of some photographer or other who had called to inquire about "that girl who modeled for Schlagel."

"They're coming after you already," he said. "I keep telling them you're busy, but sooner or later you're going to have to make up your mind about going into modeling full time or giving it up altogether. When Schlagel's cover appears, you'll have the sort of opportunity that some girls work toward for years without achieving. What you want to do about it is up to you. I could talk for three hours on the subject of why you should stay out of modeling, and for three hours more on why you ought to go in. In either case, you have the satisfaction of knowing you could start pretty far up toward the top brackets."

"I don't know yet what I want to do. I seem to be the sort of person who just isn't able to make up her mind."

"Loyalty to Jan Carter?"

"Perhaps. I know that she wouldn't want me to stay on my job if there was something better ahead for me, but I hate to leave when I've just broken in."

Bill shrugged. "I think she'd survive the shock," he said, "but it's an angle I'd rather stay out of."

The third week following Jan's illness found Cynthia busier than ever, as Bill worked overtime to meet the new deadline of the delayed catalogue. She now habitually stopped in the studio after her day's work, even when Bill did not require her to model, for she had found that there were numerous small chores about the place which she could handle quite competently, and she enjoyed being with him. Jan, of course, soon knew of this, and remarked on it, making her only approach toward what might have been construed as an allusion to their previous relationship.

"There doesn't appear to be any time for us to be together nowadays," she chided mildly one afternoon as Cynthia begged off a dinner invitation.

"Things won't always be so hectic," Cynthia replied somewhat evasively. "But Bill has been such a good friend that I want to give him whatever help I can during this rush."

And Jan smiled.

Then an odd quirk of chance stepped in to bring Cynthia squarely face to face with a situation which, she was someday to realize, was probably the turning point in her life, for in her handling of it she left her girlhood behind and became a woman. A group of Bill's photographs of another girl in riding clothes had come back rejected, and he was disgusted.

"Some literal-minded nincompoop is forgetting that these pictures are supposed to sell clothes," he said. "He wants horses in the picture. Real horses. So I guess we'll have to shoot these over, in one of the riding stables by the park."

He made arrangements with the owner of such a place, and on the afternoon of the following Saturday Cynthia and he drove over to it. There was some discussion with the owner, who was in a hurry to leave for lunch, and then Bill returned to the car to unload his equipment while Cynthia, who was already wearing the first outfit to be photographed, moved from stall to stall, bribing the horses with lumps of sugar which she was carrying.

Suddenly a noisy, thumping commotion broke out at the far end of the stable. A protesting whinny cut through a burst of profanity, and Cynthia saw a pitchfork raised high in a jabbing motion, although she could not see the figure wielding it. Anger boiled in her veins, and she moved to interfere.

"Stop that!" she exclaimed. "Stop that at once!"

She rounded the corner of the stall, and at the same instant the man turned.

It was Jake. Jake, and he recognized her instantly.

"Well, now," he said, "if it ain't our little Miss stuck-up, putting her nose in where it don't belong, just like usual." He leaned on the fork and smirked lazily. "Or maybe you just stopped by to talk over old times. Seems like I remember we got lots of things we could talk over."

His red-rimmed eyes crinkled in a lewd wink, and Cynthia felt fear strike deep into her stomach. An impulse to run out of the place almost overcame her. Momentarily, she had forgotten that Bill was somewhere nearby.

For long, tortured months her dreams had been terror-ridden by images of this man. Awake, she had often speculated on the possibility of meeting him again, and had mentally cowered at the thought. And now, as though destiny prodded her life with a cruelly jesting finger, she found him again, no less the sadistic, dimly shrewd brute she had remembered.

"Mought even say," he suggested, "that some of the things we could talk over are *private* things—not the kind of lah-de-dah talk I hear among the, what you call, fancy society people who come here to ride. Not the kind of talk, you'd maybe want to get out around your New York friends."

He laughed without mirth, and casually spat within inches of her feet, then went on,

"Well, now I'm the kind of man who can listen to reason. Say we want to keep our own business real private. I got a room where we can talk over things like that.—*Hi! Get back there!*"

The horse had moved skittishly at some motion he made. Instantly he threatened it with the fork, and the animal danced sidewise, eyes rolling. And in Cynthia, fright was swept away by the tide of rage she felt.

"I want you to stop torturing that horse!" she heard herself saying. She knew it was her voice, but she was surprised at its steadiness.

"Oh, you want, do you?" Jake said. "*You want*—you and the rest of that fancy crowd that comes here. Always so free when it comes to givin' orders, ain't we? Well listen, Miss fancy-pants, I don't take no orders from you. When I decide a horse needs a workin'-over, he gets it."

He brought the pitchfork up again, and something snapped in Cynthia like a taut cord. She took three steps forward, blindly furious, and struck out with the riding crop she carried.

Jake dropped the pitchfork and raised his hand to his neck, where the blow had fallen. On his face was an expression which indicated that he was having some difficulty in believing his own senses. He could not have been more amazed if a barn mouse had attacked him. Then he moved toward her and snatched at the riding crop.

But Cynthia was quicker, and he found it out of reach. He grabbed her other wrist and dragged her toward him, snatched again. With all her strength, then, the girl brought the riding crop in a whistling arc to his face, caught his other cheek with the returning, backhand motion. He dropped her wrist and covered his face with his hands. He stumbled back a step—and Cynthia moved forward.

All the hatred which had been gathered within her, burst like a long-festered abscess. She struck again and again and again, driving him with her sheer fury. An angry, mumbling protest worked in the man's throat as he retreated, but he found no hesitation in her, no momentary weakness in her attack as she pressed her advantage with all the strength she could summon.

He backed into the wall, lost his balance when he tried to surge forward, and went down under the sheer weight of pain that rained upon his shoulders. Then a familiar, quiet voice cut through the red mist of Cynthia's rage.

"I should say you have made your point quite clear," Bill said. He stepped between them, turned his back on Jake, and looked steadily into Cynthia's face. "It won't do much good to kill him, you know." She drew a deep, half-choked sigh and moved back, rubbing the heel of her thumb nervously over her forehead.

Behind Bill's back, Jake now swayed to his feet. He shook his head as though to clear it, then lurched toward them, striking at the girl over Bill's shoulder. Foul abuse mouthed out of him as he struggled to gain a position where he could reach her. Bill turned then, gathered the filthy shirt-front in a knotting fist and slammed him heavily against the side of the stall. Jake stood there wiping his mouth with the back of his hand, and then he reached out for the pitchfork.

"I didn't like that, mister," he said. "I've stood about all I can from you smart-aleck, New York lah-de-dahs. Now somebody's gonna get hurt."

Bill thrust Cynthia quickly away and kept Jake's attention on himself by moving as though to grasp the fork. Jake jabbed, and Bill drew back, retreating step by slow step. Jake feinted with the needle-sharp prongs again, and his yellowed teeth were uncovered in a damp grin.

"Kinda scares ya, don't it?" he chortled. "Makes ya feel kinda mushy inside when ya think what a fork can do if ya get it in the face—or in the belly—or—"

He lowered the weapon until the tines were groin-high. And then Cynthia flashed forward. Coming upon him from the side, she grasped his right arm in both of hers and clung to it, dragging it downward with her weight. He tried to shake her off, but it was like shaking a burr from a blanket. The end of the fork dropped impotently, and Bill seized the opportunity to stamp heavily upon its handle. Jake dropped it altogether and managed to fling Cynthia aside as Bill moved in.

Three times Bill struck, and the third time Jake went down and did not get up.

"I think you had better go back to the car," Bill said to Cynthia.

"I'll go when you do," she said. "I'm not afraid of him any more. Do you hear? I'm not afraid of him at all."

A third voice broke in. It was the stable owner, who had apparently stopped back on some errand, and had witnessed the last few moments.

"Great God!" he exclaimed. "I just got in on the tail end of things, but I saw enough to make *me* afraid of him." He picked up the hay-fork and put it safely out of the way. "Hey, Eddie! Frank!" he roared at the foot of the ramp leading to the upper floors. "Come down here and see if you can find that cop on the beat. I want to fire this rum-pot nut who came in last week, and I want to be sure he goes peaceably."

Bill pulled smoothly to the curb before Cynthia's apartment house. It was a warm and quiet night. They had been for a long drive in the country, had enjoyed a meal and a short interlude of dancing at a roadside inn, and had come down the West Side Highway in the jeweled glitter of early evening.

"Who was that madman?" Bill had asked once after they left the riding stable. "I've been trying to take my cues from you, but I'm still pretty much in the dark."

And Cynthia had replied, "Will it be all right if I tell you later? I feel so darned good right now that I just want to spend my time enjoying myself. You can't know how good I feel."

And so the subject of Jake was put aside, and the rest of the day was given over to the trivial things which loom so large in the bitter-sweet memories of those who have known the groping early moments of a young love.

"Please come up," Cynthia said as Bill shut off the motor. "You've never seen my place, and—we have a lot of things to talk about."

In her apartment Bill tramped about approvingly, the kitten at his heels.

"I like it," he said. "If you wanted to give some time to it, I believe you could do something as an interior decorator."

Cynthia appraised her work with a critical objectiveness. Then, surprisingly, she said,

"I know I could. I would do very well at it."

She made tea, and they sat together on the couch and laughed at the antics of the kitten, who thought he was going to grow up to be a tiger.

"He reminds me of you," Bill said as the little ball of fur snarled over his shoe. "He'll tackle anything."

Cynthia took a deep breath. The time had arrived to explain to Bill just what Jake was in her life.

"Bill," she said, looking in to the dregs of her cup. "That man today—for a life-time, it seems, I've been afraid of meeting him. I've dreaded it with the sort of dread that some people have of death, because to me he was death, of a sort. You see, he helped with the horses at the school I attended. And one night he—raped me."

She turned her eyes to Bill and searched his face. There was gravity there without shock, deep concern which was not pitying.

"I'll spare you the details," she said. "You saw what sort of brute he is, so you'll realize that it was a vicious and terrifying thing. And I've carried that memory like a stone, lived with a fear that jumped to my throat every time I saw someone who looked like him. Today I found that there was something in me that was bigger than fear, and the fear died. If he had hurt you with that pitchfork, I think—yes, I think I should have killed him—somehow."

Bill kissed her then. Kissed her quietly and with meaning, and she rested her head on his shoulder and touched his cheek.

"More," she said, relaxing against him. Their lips moved together and clung, and a deep sense of peace and rightness was hers. "I don't think I ever really enjoyed being kissed before. It's as though something bitter and smelling of sickness wasn't in me any longer." She stretched out on the couch, her torso held in Bill's embrace, and then she looked at the skylight and laughed up at the stars.

She stroked her cheek against Bill's smoke-hued tweeds. Her ear rested upon the broad frame of his chest, listening to the powerful beat of his heart. His hands moved through her golden hair, letting it slip through his fingers in luxuriant, scent-breathing masses. Now he buried his face in that silky softness, kissed her hair and her throat and her shoulders. Gently he stroked her arm, and Cynthia now heard whispered the words he had one rainy night shouted from his window:

"I love you, Cynthia."

She raised one of his hands from her breast and formed it into a fist, pressing the fingers tight until it became the maul which had driven smashingly against Jake's twisting mouth. She studied the hand, turning it from side to side, then opened the fingers again, pressed her lips upon the warm palm and kissed gentleness into it before laying it again upon her body.

"I think I love you too, Bill," she said. "I'm not sure, because it's a new feeling for me. But there is something—something I've never felt toward anyone." She raised an inch or two the skirt of the dress she had changed into at the studio, and, pointing her toe toward the corner of the room, examined the nyloned outline of one leg. "You make me aware of myself in a way that's strange to me. I'm glad for every nice thing I can find about myself and my body. I want to be nice—for you."

She laughed at the memory, and told him the nickname which she had once had.

"A short while ago I couldn't have told you that," she said. "Now—I'm rather proud of myself."

Her sun-darkened skin was like wheat where her arms and throat had been exposed. Beneath the loose bodice of her dress, as it fell back, the toasted brownness melted into a creamy light gold. On her flesh his fingertips were light and warm as they moved caressingly over the splendid swells and softnesses. The kitten eyed the movement of his hand beneath the thin fabric, stalked it ferociously, and leaped.

"I think there are too many people on this couch," Bill objected.

"I'll get rid of him," Cynthia said. Rising from the couch, she gathered the embryo warrior in her arms and took him into the other room. She was gone for several minutes, and when she returned, closing the door behind her, she was wearing a loose, and very sheer, black negligee.

"Isn't it silly?" she asked, pirouetting to bloom the skirt in a billowing circle. "I was feeling very sophisticated the day I bought it, and after I tried it on once I never wore it."

"It's silly," Bill admitted, "but I like it. I guess I like it because it almost isn't there at all."

"It calls for soft lights," Cynthia said. "So, if you don't mind, I'll turn on the mystery. I do *so* want to be a *femme fatale*."

She switched off the electric bulbs and lighted two sturdy red candles at either end of the mantle-piece. Double shadows leaped into being on the opposite wall, and she called Bill to come and stand beside her.

"You're a giant," she decided, watching the flickering silhouettes. "But a very benevolent and nice giant. The goblins are all gone."

Bill swept her up and held her in his arms. She lost herself in his kiss. He carried her to the couch and knelt beside her, covering her with a rain of kisses which knew no refusal. The shadowed mysteries of her body, half revealed by the thin, black wispiness of her negligee, pressed back against the stroke of his cheek as Cynthia ran her fingers through his crisping hair. That burning tide which his caress had once before caused to stir in her swept upward again—and this time the wall crumbled before it. Bill murmured in her ear, in words only half heard, but wholly understood, so that she need only murmur back, "Yes, Bill darling, yes…"

Then, with a wild, glad cry which was half a sob tom from the ache of beauty, he was beside her, plunging to her love. And eagerly she came to him, flinging her heart into his, and her mouth beneath his kiss was laughing and glad, and her body sang.

CHAPTER FIFTEEN

"I'M going to ask for a vacation," Cynthia said. And then she added, "From you."

Bill paused with his fork halfway to his mouth. "Hey!" he protested.

"That's right," she insisted. "I've been seeing no one but you for the last three weeks, and some very important things have happened to me, without me being able to sit down quietly and figure out what they all mean."

It was their noon hour midway into the week which followed Cynthia 's encounter with Jake. Cynthia looked around the crowded cafeteria.

"No more lunches here for awhile," she said. "The catalogue job is all wrapped up, so you don't need me for that. For a few days I just want to go to work and then go home and sit by myself."

"Divorced before I'm even married," Bill grumbled. "I might have known you were too good to last."

"That's exactly why I want to be alone," Cynthia said. "I want this to last, but I'm still not sure of myself, and I don't want us to find ourselves in some sort of a stew just because we didn't stop to learn how we really felt about each other. I think I want to be with you for the rest of always, but I've never been in love with a man before. Maybe part of it is just relief to learn you're not another Jake. A lot of it must be gratitude for the good things you've brought into my life—and you wouldn't want me to stay with you out of gratitude."

"All right," Bill said. "Go off to commune with yourself in the wilderness of Greenwich Village. But I'm not going to enjoy it."

So, for the following several days, Cynthia became a part-time hermit. Books engaged a large measure of her interest, especially those having to do with design and home decoration, for she was curious to see just how far her bent in that direction might be cultivated. She was, it is true, lonely a large part of the time, and a short phone call from Bill each evening became a small ritual to which she looked forward. But, scorning the temptation to see him, she accepted that loneliness as part of a period of self-discipline, and when she sought entertainment of any sort outside herself, it was only to go alone to a lecture or, in extremity, a motion picture. If she had, during this period, any relationship approaching closer than the most casual passing of the time of day, it was with her next-door neighbor, an odd, bird-like old maid who, on the pretext of borrowing a cup of sugar, would settle herself and gossip on matters so far removed from Cynthia's concerns that their very pettiness made them a refreshing interlude. And then even that inconsequential contact was discontinued, for someone bought up the woman's lease, under circumstances which she made so mysterious that one gathered she was dealing with a gang of counterfeiters. Within a matter of days she moved out, the counterfeiters, or whoever they might be, made no sociable overtures, and Cynthia was as close as she could ever be to the solitude she thought her problems demanded.

Her relationship with Jan became, during this period, a strange and remote watchfulness on both sides. Like armies in truce they met and discussed their affairs of business with impersonal, disciplined courtesy. If there was in Jan any urge to renew their intimacy, she kept any evidence of it well in check, and it was Cynthia, finally who reluctantly gave, slightly, under pressure of the situation.

"I'm playing Gautama under the fig tree or whatever it was," she explained to Jan one day. "When I come back out I expect to be full of answers about everything. Especially about me, and what makes me tick."

"I hope they are happy answers," Jan said. And that was all. She displayed no prying curiosity, asked no questions. She seemed content that Cynthia should be working out her own problems in her own way, and Cynthia was grateful that she showed no disposition to interfere. Whatever else Jan Carter might be Cynthia knew that in some aspects of her character she was the most understanding and undemanding personality one might encounter in a lifetime.

It was with considerable surprise, then, that Cynthia answered her phone early one evening and found Jan on the wire.

"I'm sorry to break in on your meditations this way," Jan apologized, "but something has just developed which means I'll be—out of town for a few days. It promises to be such a dull trip that I hoped we could get together this evening, so I'll have something pleasant to think about while I'm gone."

"Why—of course," Cynthia said, hoping that her reluctance was not obvious. "I think it's about time I was able to move about a bit and take a little nourishing broth."

The fact that she did feel reluctance gave her a twinge of conscience. From their first meeting Jan had been a kind and strengthening friend, and if the product of that friendship had been an initiation into perverted and barren ways—well, Cynthia knew how Jan must have struggled against herself, and knew also that what had been between them had been, in its fashion, a thing of love, twisted and erratic though that love might be.

"I have to make a stop at the office," Jan said. "Suppose we meet there in—half an hour?"

"Half an hour," Cynthia repeated. "I'll be the girl with moss growing up her trunk."

But when a dozen suddenly remembered household tasks were put out of the way, when she had fed the kitten and showered and dressed, she had trouble finding a cab, and the one she finally did get blew a tire, so that it was much more than half an hour before she saw Jan, and in that time a great deal had happened.

"Hello," Jan said. "I saw your office light and thought I might find Cynthia here, since I'm a bit late for our appointment."

Bill ran his fingers through his hair and said, "I've hardly seen Cynthia for several days. I thought she wasn't seeing anyone."

"I broke through the veil of silence tonight. But even before this retreat of hers. I was seeing very little of her. Tell me, do you work *every* night?"

"Not at all. When Cynthia was modeling, we worked nights because that was when she was free. Tonight I'm just playing, doing experimental stuff. Thank heaven I work at something I enjoy."

He motioned Jan to a chair and took one himself. He held flame to her cigaret and to his own, and then he asked,

"Do you enjoy your work?"

"No," Jan replied. "Not particularly. Some of it is—anything but enjoyable."

"You really feel that way about it?"

"I very seldom say things I don't mean."

"Then you won't feel too badly about giving it up."

"Giving it up? Who said anything about giving it up?"

"I did. Somehow I believe that the House of Cimier is going to close its doors before long. I meant to see you about that in a day or two."

Jan cocked her head in puzzlement, and laughed.

"This is a very odd and interesting conversation. Why in the world should you think I'm going out of business?"

"Because I don't think the profitable end of your business is a very nice business for anyone to be in. And if Cynthia is going to continue to work for you, I'd like to see that branch of your business discontinued."

Jan's mouth tightened, and her eyes narrowed by a hair's breadth.

"I suppose you'll explain that remark," she said.

"I shall. Take a look at this. I think you'll find it interesting."

From his desk he took a loose-leaf binder and passed it to her. In it, mounted on sheets, were several photographs, with dates written in next to them. Beneath each picture was pasted either a newspaper clipping or a typewritten notation.

"Credit for the pictures," Bill said, "belongs to a young fellow I hired to sit in a window on the opposite corner and take a telephoto shot of everyone he saw entering or leaving your place. Identifying the people was pretty tough, and sometimes impossible, but the social editors of a couple of newspapers helped a lot. Now look at the clippings and the dates. There is a strange coincidence amongst them, don't you think? Mrs. So-and-So, who is not one of your regular customers, is seen entering your building on such-and-such a date. Within a day or so a gossip column mentions in passing that she is recuperating from 'flu,' or is traveling in Bermuda, or is simply 'resting'. The typewritten notes indicate the sort of answers I got when I posed as a news-hound and called the homes of some of these women. Mrs. So-and-So is not at home. Miss So-and-So is out of town. And so on. Need I go into further detail, or will you concede me this point?"

"A very neat job of sleuthing," Jan said. "Without conceding anything, I should like to know what your conclusion may be and what you intend to do about it."

"The conclusion is obvious. What I intend to do is ask that you accept the simple existence of this evidence as one hell of a good reason for you to close up shop. I know that you can't be running a thing like this without some heavy protection from above—and I think I know where it's coming from. But there are still a few decent newspapers in this town, and if they're given a lead, I believe they can uncover the tie-in. If not, you may have to take the rap alone... Because, believe me, when a few of your clients are confronted with the possibility of having material like this publicized, they'll be only too happy to rat in order to save their own skins."

"Why, exactly, are you so much interested in something which doesn't concern you?"

"It does concern me, because it concerns Cynthia. I don't want to see her mixed up with anything like this, even though I know you're only using her as part of the front."

"Have you discussed this with her?"

"No. And I'd rather not. I know that in the past she has placed a lot of faith in you, and I see nothing to be gained by telling her, right now, what your business really is."

"You appear to be quite certain that you know best what is good for Cynthia."

"I'll be quite frank. I know that, under no circumstances is a woman like you a good thing for a girl like Cynthia. I think she has enough innate good sense to eventually draw away from your influence, but I believe that in the meantime you can do her a great deal of harm."

"Come, now. Aren't you letting your personal feelings interfere with your own good sense? You must by this time know that any harm which has come to her in the past has not been as a result of any influence of mine, but simply the outgrowth of some hellishly unfortunate experiences with men. You see, I happen to love that girl, and I refuse to believe that, despite all the problems which lie in the path of a love like mine, any experience she might have with me would leave her the sick, scared pup she was when I met her. It took a man to do that, and if she has been driven away from men, it was a man who did it, and not I."

"You are speaking rather more openly about yourself than I expected," Bill said.

"There's no point in being squeamish about a matter which we both know to be a fact. Aside from your interest in my business affairs, and in my strictly personal concern with Cynthia, the worst thing you seem able to say about me is that I am a Lesbian, and in view of the evidence, I can't say I believe it to be such a terrible thing as you'd like to assume. The worst thing I can say about you is that you're a man, so we're stalemated."

Bill laughed, though his amusement was tinged with an ironical rejection of her words.

"Your danger to Cynthia," he replied, "lies exactly in the fact that you are such an admirable personality in so many ways. A lesser person could not influence her so greatly—and I know that your influence is wrong for her."

"I believe Cynthia should be allowed to make her own decision on that subject. But I realize, of course, that you intend to bring certain other pressures to bear. This little book of yours ought to be a very powerful weapon in your campaign to make her dislike me."

Bill shook his head as he took back the binder and returned it to his desk. "I don't intend to use it that way. If you want to play a man's game—well, I think I'm a better man than you any day in the week and six times on Sundays."

Jan's brows went up, and the corners of her mouth twitched into a smile.

"So it's war," she agreed. "Now what?"

"I'll begin," Bill said, "by asking Cynthia to break her date with you this evening and go out with me. And not simply to show off, either. I don't know what sort of an evening you had planned, but I do know that, whatever it is, I'm against it. I simply don't want her in your company. As for your sideline—I'm only asking you—telling you—to close it. Aside from all questions of right and wrong, which I won't even attempt to argue with you,

I object as a tax-payer to having my money spent to finance a racket like that. I told you that I think I know who is behind you. The material I have now isn't proof of that, but I believe that proof would turn up if someone really went to work on it. Just tell *him* that the buggy-ride is over."

Just like that, Jan was thinking. Tell *him* that, knowing he'll believe I'm just trying to run out...

Aloud, she said, "I suppose there's nothing else I can do. But I have one more customer whom I absolutely have to accept. I promised her, and she is a very important customer to me."

"No one is that important. Turn her down."

"I can't. No, I really can't. You see, I'm the customer."

"You? *You?*"

"Crazy, isn't it? And it doesn't fit in at all with what you know about me. But I shouldn't try to understand it if I were you."

Cynthia entered the studio door just then.

"What have you two been up to?" she demanded. "Through the window you looked as though you might be plotting the revolution."

"Nothing so drastic," Bill smiled. "Say, you're looking wonderful! How about going out with me this evening, so I can show you off? Let's do something worthless for a change, like driving to a lake and dancing."

"Oh Bill, I'm sorry," Cynthia said with genuine regret. "I thought you knew I had a date with Jan."

Bill turned and looked at Jan. I'm sure Miss Carter wouldn't hold you to that," he said.

"By no means," Jan agreed.

"I—oh golly, I don't know what to say," Cynthia frowned. "Was it very important about tonight, Jan? I mean, was there anything special you wanted to do?"

Jan dismissed the possibility with a light toss of her head.

"Perhaps," Bill suggested, "Perhaps Jan would like to come with us?"

"Fie on your carousal," Jan laughed. "I have better things to do than watch an empty jigging."

"Well—if we could make it another night, Jan? Would you mind very much?"

"I should mind very much feeling that you had ever in your life done anything you didn't want to do, because of me," Jan said.

Those were the last words, save only three, which she was ever to address directly to Cynthia. She stood up and grinned with cheerful wryness at Bill.

"Your round," she told him.

Then she took Cynthia's hand and held it warmly in hers for a moment, searching Cynthia's face with her eyes.

"Goodby, my love," she whispered.

She turned her back on them and walked out the door toward an appointment she had with Death.

CHAPTER SIXTEEN

O N Monday, when she went to work, Cynthia was mulling over the question of leaving her job. She was sure that she could do better as a model, but further than that, she felt that modeling would allow her more free time to work toward interior decoration, which she now believed would be her eventual field. She decided to talk it over with Jan at the first opportunity, for she knew that Jan's advice would be unprejudiced by any thought of trying to hold her there against her best interest.

Jan was not there on that day, nor had Cynthia expected her to be, although she did not know how long Jan had planned to be away. Dr. Ramsey appeared as a part of her regular routine, and Meg was unpleasant, which was also routine. On Tuesday Dr. Ramsey also appeared, which was unusual, but not unprecedented, and Cynthia took advantage of the circumstance to ask if she had any idea as to when Jan might return. The reply was a curt, if not quite discourteous, negative. Something was obviously preying on Dr. Ramsey's mind, and Cynthia privately reflected that even psychiatrists were sometimes unable to control their responses to the worrisome things of life.

By Wednesday morning Meg was so completely unbearable that Cynthia kept out of her way as much as possible. If matters there grew much worse, Cynthia told herself, there would be nothing to discuss with Jan, for it would simply be impossible to work in the same building with the girl.

And on that day it happened.

Just as she was going out to lunch, Cynthia almost bumped into a large, well-groomed man of middle age whose face seemed familiar, although she could not remember having met him before. That, in addition to the fact that a man in the House of Cimier was somewhat of a rarity, led her to stare after him as he went directly to Dr. Ramsey and entered a quiet conversation with her. He glanced at her once, with apparent recognition in his china-blue eyes, but she still could not place him, and during her meal with Bill she forgot the incident.

But, as she and Bill came up the street an hour later, she somehow immediately connected the man with the commotion which was taking place about the big brownstone. A crowd was milling around, police cars and an ambulance were drawn up, and news photographers were fighting their way back and forth, photographing everything in sight.

"There's been a street accident," Bill suggested. "Shall we walk back in a few minutes?"

"Something's happened at the place," Cynthia contradicted. "See how they're all crowded around the doorways?"

They pushed into the fringe of the mob, and Bill button-holed three men before he found one who seemed to have any idea of what had happened.

"Murder," the man said happily. "Woman shot a man."

"Yeah, but you know *who* she shot?" put in another, who had overheard. One of your big-shot politicians." And he named—*him.*

"Bill," Cynthia exclaimed, grasping his arm. "That's the man I saw going in just as I was leaving! I knew his face was familiar."

"You saw *him* going in there?" Bill asked in a low tone. "Good God! Let's see what else we can learn. But wait—don't mention to anyone that you work here. They may be detaining everyone connected with the place."

Bill found a press photographer he knew and took him aside.

"What's the story on this?" he asked. "I seem to have been out to lunch at the wrong time."

"Right next to your joint, huh Bill? Maybe I can get part of your building into one of my shots. Good publicity."

"Never mind that. What happened?"

"Oh, that. Well, the old nickle-grabber finally got his, all right. Shot deader than yesterday's paper by that woman—what's the name … Carter, yeah, Carter. The dame that runs the place."

"But she couldn't have!" Cynthia broke in. "She's—I mean, I heard she was out of town when it happened."

"Well, that may be what you heard, miss, but the woman I was taking pictures of in that hospital bed is supposed to be her."

"What hospital bed?" Bill demanded. "Was she injured too?"

The man looked at Cynthia, apparently decided that she was too young to hear all he knew, and said, "Well, it's kind of a funny thing, Bill. There's all sorts of rumors flying around, but I wouldn't say she was exactly injured. You know, most of that top floor is rigged up like a hospital, only the people who work in the place all claim they never heard of such a thing. All except that woman doctor, and she's not saying anything. Anyway, there's something real fishy about the set-up, and it's a pretty sure thing the Big Shot was in right up to his neck. Somebody has it figured that he heard she was dying—"

"Dying?" Cynthia whispered.

"Yeah. Of that purple fever or whatever you call it. So he runs over to straighten out their business affairs before she kicks the bucket. But instead, she straightens him out with a slug from the gat she had in the bedside table. Only here's the craziest thing of all. Some cleaning woman was going by the door when the shot was fired, and you know what she said, that Carter dame, just before she shot him? She yells, 'Hey, Superman, I've got news for you. My gun shoots real bullets.' And then she laughs."

"Bill. Take me home."

"Yeah," said the photographer, "makes you sick to think what some people will do don't it? But I guess they never will know why she did it, because she was unconscious when they took her away to the hospital, and a doc I talked to said he didn't think she'd come out of it, so it wouldn't be any use trying to talk to her."

In her apartment, Cynthia sat and stared in stony silence at the wall, a silence which all Bill's efforts had been for almost an hour unable to break through. The kitten pushed a magazine across the floor, and Bill said absently,

"Your cover will be on the stands tomorrow morning."

And for some reason, that broke the silence.

"I don't want my picture on a magazine," Cynthia said. "I don't want this apartment and I don't want you and I don't think I want to live. All I want is to have Jan back, alive and fun, the way she was, just have her walk in this room and say it was all some horrible mistake, and please, God, let her just do that, and I'll love her and stay with her always, the way I said I would once, only I was lying."

"Cynthia..."

"She wanted to see me the other night, before she went off by herself to have *that* done. And I went dancing with you. I went dancing with you!"

She turned on him suddenly and said, "You knew what was going on in that place. You even knew, or guessed, who was in it with her. How much more did you know? Did you know she was going to have that done?"

"Yes, Cynthia, I did. I didn't know when."

"And you didn't tell me! You and I went off to dance, while she went off to die!"

"I'm sure that she felt perfectly safe. Jan was no fool about things like that. And she didn't want you to know, or she'd have told you."

"I don't think I want you to be here now. Will you go away, please?"

"I don't want to leave you in this state."

"You needn't concern yourself—I won't do anything drastic. I'm not brave enough to die. And please don't try to see me."

He went to the door reluctantly.

"I'll phone later tonight," he said quietly.

"Yes, do that. Phone, and perhaps we'll go dancing. Maybe we can make a date to go out some night next week and dance on Jan's grave!"

Two nights later Cynthia's bell rang, and she opened the door to find Meg.

"May I come in?" she asked sullenly. "I wouldn't be here, but Jan made me promise I'd come."

"Of course," Cynthia said, and guided her to a chair. "You promised Jan? Then you must have been with her ... "

"I was with her for three nights in that place, as soon as I learned from Dr. Ramsey that she was there and wasn't doing well."

"Oh why didn't you tell me!" Cynthia cried. "If I could have been with her then—if I could have helped her—"

"She didn't want you to know she was there. She didn't want you to see her ... like that. I think she knew sooner than any-one else that she was going to die. But she talked about you. She talked about you a lot."

"What did she say?" Cynthia begged. "Tell me, tell me what she said!"

Meg started to speak, stopped, and took a deep breath.

"I can't do what I meant to," she said. "I came here intending to lie to you, to tell you that she felt about you as I feel about you, because I would like to see you hurt, now. But I can't do that to Jan. She wasn't like that. She loved you. Yes, she loved you in a way I wish she had been able to love me. And her concern was to see you happy, not to own you. She wanted you—I *know* she wanted you to be happy with Bill Barton, even if it meant giving you up. But mostly she talked about the things you had done together, and she remembered them as fun, and she was happiest at those times. And she gave me this to give to you."

Rummaging in her purse, she took out a small, round object and handed it to Cynthia. It was an agate marble, dark brown, and flecked with little half-moons of gold.

"She said she'd come across it recently and thought it would make a nice ring for you. She meant to give it to you on the last night she saw you, but you apparently didn't have time for her. She said to tell you she'd had it since she was—yes, she said a little *boy*—and that it was the best damn taw on the block."

She stood up. "And that's all Jan had to say to you. But there's something I'd like to say for myself. She was delirious at times, and she talked about things she'd never have mentioned otherwise. I know who made her pregnant and I know the conditions under which she became pregnant, and I know why she shot him. And I can tell you that when she gave herself to that beast she did it because she thought she was protecting you. If anyone in this world is responsible for Jan Carter's death, you are that girl."

Cynthia's face went white, and her eyes became horrible pits of anguish. Then she shook her head, and the pain died in her.

"No," she said. "I won't carry a burden like that for the rest of my life. I can't be responsible for something I never even heard of until now. If Jan made that sort of mistake, I can only say that I understand how she could have made it, but I will not let the guilt for her death rest on my shoulders. Nor, as you know, would Jan have wanted it to."

She showed Meg to the door a few minutes afterward, and then sat down, rolling and rolling an agate marble in her palm.

Days went by, and Cynthia scarcely moved from the house. Bill's phone calls were regular bits of her evenings, and by degrees these grew more lengthy as her interest in the things he had to tell her became more normal. Then, one day while she was coming home with a bundle of groceries, she remembered something which she had done with Jan, and she found herself laughing. She stopped in the street and thought about the incident at some greater length and it still seemed funny. She was, she realized, thinking of Jan without suffering the dull ache of loss which had at first become a part of those memories. She hurried on home, and then on impulse called Bill—not without some attendant difficulties, for his number had evidently been changed.

"This is—this is Bubs," she said when she heard his voice. "When are you going to come and see me?"

"You'll know when I arrive," he promised. "Sooner than you expect."

Humming to herself, Cynthia went about the apartment, filling in time with almost anything she could find to keep herself busy. Her mind felt clear and free again, and if there was any annoyance in her world, it was a sharp, chipping thump which had begun in the apartment of the "counterfeiters" as she habitually thought of whoever it was who now occupied the place next to hers.

Gradually it was forced upon her attention that the pounding next door was something more than the mere hanging of a picture. The intervening wall began to shake, and small objects in her own room began to dance about. Then a flake of plaster fell from her side of the wall. She went over to the partition and banged it with her fist.

"Hey over there!" she shouted. "Take it easy!"

There was no answer. If anything, the hammering was louder than before, and now a large section of plaster gave way and fell. Setting her jaw, she went out into the hall and jabbed her neighbor's bell insistently.

The pounding stopped. The door opened. It was Bill.

"You!" she exclaimed.

"Weren't you expecting me?"

"Yes, but not here."

"Oh, I'm an old tenant. I just forgot to tell you."

"Well, will you please stop breaking down my wall?"

"I will not. I have permission from the landlord to put a door through here. I explained that we were getting married and wanted to live together. We are, aren't we?"

"I don't know yet. Come on over to my place and we'll talk it over."

And talk they did, for a while, but finally there was silence in that room, save for the rattle of a marble as a youthful cat chased it about the floor.

Next day Cynthia retrieved the marble from beneath a radiator and put it carefully away. Some few years later a small boy with Cynthia's eyes and Bill's chin came across it as he curiously rummaged through a box in an attic. His mother held it then, for a moment, rolling it on her palm, her eyes looking into the past and smiling. And then, because she was a wise woman who knew the value of many things, she gave it to the boy, who stuffed it in his pocket and took it outside to play, where he promptly, and properly, lost it.

THE END